The Love Ring

Alan Horn

The Love Ring

Book and Cover design by Aerophyte

ISBN: 9781520579542

FIRST EDITION: MARCH 2017

10 9 8 7 6 5 4 3 2 1

The Love Ring

Suzanne never feared her visions and they became important to her life. But when she put the love ring of Asmodeus on her finger it exposed her to modern day witches and wizards hidden among us. The Magician's Guild welcomes her and teaches her how to use her talent. But the unintended consequences of her growth are danger, fulfillment, love and the joy of submission.

Asmodeus' ring frees her to love as she has always knew she could. The unleashed carnality of her libido forces her to actualize her deepest fantasy. She reveals her ultimately submissive nature and submits to the one man she will obey. Her unique talent permits his team of adepts to recover stolen nuclear weapons from the dictator who would threaten the world. Driven by her passion, she takes the ultimate risk and publicly subjugates herself to her master without knowing whether he will take her.

Part 1 : Discovery

Chapter 1

I'm Suzy Ryder and I'm a private investigator. Most PIs start as cops or lawyers or something to do with criminals. I started because I get visions. I find things, people, pets, stolen you-name-its because I can see where they are, in a limited way. My assistant is Lucifer. Lucifer looks like a cat. I'm no longer sure. He goes with me everywhere. I've locked him in the house, in a cage, in my car. He always escapes. He's proved to be surprisingly useful so I stopped trying to leave him behind.

I got a new missing person case this morning. She vanished from the church on Friday right before the ceremony. Probably just cold feet, but her parents and friends are worried. The bride's name was Melanie Billings. Her parents and fiancé had come to my office yesterday. They wanted me to find her. The police wouldn't open a missing person file until 24 hours had passed. The fiancé wanted me to bring her back to the church. The parents just wanted her found. Three days ago Everyone was at the church. Her bridesmaids had gotten her dressed. She was alone in the prep room. The march started and nothing happened. Her mother and father went to check on her and she was gone. Bride, bouquet, and overnight bag.

I once had a fiancé and almost got married. I hadn't gotten as far as Melanie. We had set a date and making a guest list. We were talking to churches and pastors. Then I found Donald, the love of my life, in bed with my best friend, Shelly Arnesen. I screamed in rage and betrayal. He blushed and hid under the covers. My best friend was matter of fact. Shelly said, "Suzy, he isn't right for you. You should be glad I've shown you the light."

She was right. She probably did me a big favor. Don and I had great sex and some good times, but I think now we were not intimate. I don't think we ever clicked. We were friendly strangers.

She is still definitely off my Christmas card list.

I told Lucifer on him. The doctor said it looked like a lion had mauled him. He survived but he's developed a cat allergy.

I'm Suzanne Ryder, P.I. The tabloids call me the Psychic PI. I've always been good at finding lost things. Well, I am good at it. I've only failed once and it wasn't my fault. His small plane exploded when he flew into a mountain and there weren't any pieces big enough to see. They found the wreckage six months later, after the snow melted. I goofed just one time and told a reporter I could just see them in my head.

When people ask me about it I just tell them the reporter misunderstood me. My stock answer is, "I rely on thorough investigation to do my job."

I never, ever mention my mother. I think she's was a witch and I must have inherited a little of her power. I watched her make it rain from a clear sky when her garden needed watering. It was a light rain and only wet our block. I asked her about it. She only said these pesky northwest microclimates are unpredictable. Then there was the rabbit that kept getting in her garden and she turned it into a turtle. I swear, I watched her. She just said I must have been mistaken. I still had to take the turtle to the pond in the park. She could do incredible things but never showed me how. She wanted me to be an upstanding citizen and rely on my brains. She said magic was a poor way to make a living.

When I moved out to go to school Lucifer came with me. He was living with us as long as I can remember, and I'm almost thirty. He must be at least that old, but he looks like he's 3 or 4 at most. He goes everywhere with me. I mean everywhere. I lock him in the house when I go to work and he's in the car when I get there. If I lock him outside, he'll be sitting on my desk waiting for me when I get inside. He is magical. I took him to the vet just after I started at the U. The vet and assistant ran out of the exam room and told me they couldn't work on him. They never said why but they looked scared. Anyway, he understands me. If I tell him to do something, he runs off and somehow does it.

I became a Private Investigator after graduating. I had a combined psychology/business degree. After I graduated I took a job in HR at Microsoft. It was an OK job. But my visions kicked into high gear about then. I learned that if I looked at a person's resume or anything they touched, like a piece of paper or a water bottle, and closed my eyes, I got a vision of them. A video looking over their shoulder. I could see and hear them. It would last until I opened my eyes. If I had the stuff from several people in front of me, it was random who I'd see. I started doing this on all the people I interviewed and I made several decisions not to hire someone because of their comments. "Weasel" indeed. I learned I could find lost objects too. My first object was my car. I had put it in a huge twisty parking structure at Bellevue square and forgot where. Mostly as a lark I stared at my car keys and closed my eye. I got a perfect vision that showed me my car and the structure floor and row.

My "visions" just happen. I look at a clue and touch it if possible, close my eyes and draw a mental picture of whatever and the real thing appears. They always came when I needed one, but they're always just a vignette, a clue. I have to figure out all the details. I wanted to improve my abilities so I begged mom for help. She said she'd never had visions so didn't know what to do.

My mother and father were both witches and I guess its just a genetic thing. Mom always said that being a witch is no bed of roses and I should use my mind instead of magic, when I brought it up. Mom and Dad were 'closet' witches. They would never speak of it and when I caught them in something impossible they would just say it was my imagination. I don't think they remembered how curious and sneaky children can be. I caught them doing something impossible a couple of times before they would talk to me about it at all. I saw Dad fall off a ladder when he was cleaning a gutter and he stopped falling six feet off the ground and lowered himself down and saw me standing at the corner of he house with my mouth open.; He said something like, "Strong winds today. be careful." He wouldn't say anything else, ever. Mom showed me a few things, but she never gave clear directions. Usually her fuzzy directions made for nothing happening. There were a few nasty surprises along the way so I learned to be careful in trying new things. My intentions were always good. I tried to cure Mrs. Gummidge's cat of mange. Before they caught the confused but happy lion, he had eaten three stray dogs. Scared Mrs. Gummidge half to death.

Dad and Mom's skills were different. Maybe gender linked. She could read people and change their feelings. She was a healer and a grower. Dad was a fixer, he could tell how well a thing was working by looking at it. He was the only adult I ever say that could program a TV/VCR/DVD remote. He is very strong and seems almost invulnerable. We were together downtown and a car hit him. The car was dented n and wouldn't run. My father helped get the driver out of the car. I'm lucky he was between the car and me. Now I understand he had a strong shield.

Oh, and they can fly. One night when I was twelve and supposed to be spending the night with a friend, she got sick and I came home early. It was dark and I saw them play, playing over the monkey puzzle tree in our back yard. They were like to really big sparrows darting around the branches. I watched them for ten minutes before I went inside and turned on a light. My emotions were askew. Kids don't think of their parents as frolicking or exuberant. They are the steady ones that keep the sun rising in the morning. My parents were cavorting in the leaves live chimps in the zoo. And they were fucking flying. That was impossible. Except that I watched them for minutes. I felt cheated, lied to. They had this wonderful ability and never showed me how to do it. I felt literally down cast. Cast down to earth while they played in the sky.

I read everything I could find, but I never found anything useful. The stories are full of descriptions of fantastic books of spells. They always need hard to find ingredients. Eye of Newt, Hummingbird nose hairs, Fried snail's testicles, and so on. Never saw a clear book or any of those ingredients.

I had all I needed so I tried to get a vision of Melanie. Lucifer did his part, he sat on my lap and purred. The parents gave me some of her clothes and the fiancé gave me a book she liked. I got my retainer and they left. I handled all the things and sure enough I got a vision. As usual, I saw just enough for a clue. I saw her in a cab. I could see the name on the cab and part of its license plate. I had worked with that company before. They told me the cab took her to a corner in Tukwila, only twenty minutes away if its not rush hour. I got my purse and Lucifer was in the car before I got there. Magic, I swear.

It was a light industrial neighborhood with low offices and light manufacturing. There was a chain hotel on the corner so I started there. Lucifer went with me. Before I opened the door, I told him, I need Melanie's room number. So I talked to the clerk, named Singh, according to his badge and showed him Melanie's photo. He told me he hadn't seen her and he didn't work all day yesterday so he might not have seen her. I think he just wanted a bribe.

I thought about it when Lucifer appeared at my feet holding a room key in his mouth. I thanked Singh and told him I just remembered her room. I picked up the key from Lucifer and went up the stairs to the second floor. Lucifer was waiting for me in front of room 215.

I knocked but got no answer. I tried the key and found Melanie lying on the bed, next to a Latino man about her age. They were both dressed.

"Hi, Melanie," I said.

The guy jumped off the bed and came toward me. He growled, "Get the fuck out of our room."

Lucifer didn't like his attitude and he roared like an adult lion. I jumped and the guy stopped so hard he fell back on his bottom. He was white as a corpse.

I reached behind me and pulled the Glock 17 out of my waistband and showed it to him. I didn't point it at him. Yet. In my ugliest voice I yelled, "Stop or I'll shoot. I'm a licensed Private Investigator and I have a permit for this gun. Did you kidnap Ms. Billings?"

I was pretty sure he hadn't but he didn't know that.

He jumped back up and sat on the bed. He didn't even look at my gun. He yelled, "What. No. She didn't want to marry that guy. She asked me to help her! Did you bring a fricking lion with you?"

I snarled, "He a sweet kitty unless someone threatens me. Now talk calmly and don't startle him."

I put the gun away. I said to Melanie, "You've worried your parents. Do you want to stay here?"

Melanie nodded her head and said, "Y..Yes. I didn't know what to do. I panicked and ran. I called Rafael and he met me here."

I switched to my soothing voice and said, "OK. Call them and tell them you're OK. They are quite worried. Now."

Melanie called. I listened for a minute then left. Lucifer was in the car before I got there, looking smug and grooming his paw. I had closed the car windows and locked the doors.

Chapter 2

I drove back to my office.

Gus was sitting in an easy chair in the outer office reading 'Guns & Ammo.' Gus is my backup for risky jobs. He's big and tough. His size intimidates most would be assailants. Former SEAL and cop, now retired. He's the sort of gruff, kindly, loving protector that wouldn't leave an enemy alive to try again. Gus doesn't have any relatives left alive and neither do I. He's sort of adopted me. I loved my father and mother, but Gus would have been great too.

I said, "Gus, looking to upgrade?"

He grinned and said, 'Nah. Just keeping current."

Millie was my office manager. She was a Skallam Indian and knows more about the woods around here than any white man. Her full name is Millicent Tsosie and she managed things with an iron fist. She may have worked for me, but I did what she said in here.

I said, "Hi Millie. I found Melanie Billings. She just got cold feet and didn't know how to tell anyone, so she ran away."

Millie said, "Great. If you give me the expense sheet today, I can close that file." She handed me a couple of message slips

"Yes, Millie," I said and went into the kitchen to get a cup of coffee. I like mine strong. I bought the office one of those cup at a time machines. The prepackaged cartridges everyone sells nowadays were far to weak for me. I found a plastic cartridge on line. I can fill it with enough coffee to make a cup strong enough for me. It was the only way I could get mine strong enough without poisoning everyone else. I got the habit from my father. He said coffee comes in several grades. He called them Joe, coffee, java, rocket fuel, and carbon remover. I liked Rocket Fuel. I have another machine at home.

I heard the outside door open and peeked out. It was our mailman, Billy. He was as gay as a clam. He stopped in front of Gus and said, in a soft voice, "Hi Gus. How are you?"

Gus looked up from his magazine and saw it was Billy. He growled. "I'm OK. I'm busy." and he looked back down.

Billy didn't seem to notice Gus' attitude and said, "That's nice." and went to Millie. He handed her a large manila envelope and said, "Special delivery. You need to sign for it."

Millie looked at it, signed the green card and handed the package back to Billy. He removed the green card and gave the package back to Millie. He spun on his heel and left. He glanced at Gus as he walked to the door.

Millie looked at me and said, "Got a package from the prosecutor."

"Which prosecutor," I asked?

"County."

"Let's see it," I said."

She handed me a thin manila envelope, mailed today I saw. I ripped it open. There was a letter requesting my services at market rate. I read through a couple of pages. It seemed the accused in a criminal case had gone missing. His name was Ralph Henry. He was 46, divorced with one child, James, grown and living in Los Angeles. He had shot a store clerk during a robbery. She died instantly. Ralph had escaped by jumping out of a third story window onto the awning of a vendor's cart on the street. He had emptied his bank account and gone. They wanted me to locate him. He had an arrest warrant open but no idea where to serve it. They thought he was out of the state. They'd even included a check for a retainer. "Millie," I said, " they want me to find a missing murderer. Send them a response that I'll take the case and ask them to send me some thing he's handled or worn. Tell them I'd like it ASAP."

I thought about that and said, "No, don't send them a letter, call them and tell them I want to get something today."

Millie said, "Got it." She picked up her phone.

"Gus, you busy?

"Nope, want me to go with you?"

"No. I'm not going anywhere now. If they give Millie something, would you go get it?"

"Sure."

I went into my office and found Lucifer curled up in his favorite chair. I needed to write a report for Mr. and Mrs. Billings and fill out my expense log for the case. I opened the top, left hand drawer and heard something flutter off the back end and slide to the bottom. Shoot. I had been meaning to clean out the drawer before this. Too late. I pulled out the bottom drawer and shone a light into the hole. The desk had been my parents and I just had it moved to my office. There was the note pad that had fallen, a few coins and a white envelope. I fished everything out. 23 cents, my note pad, and an envelope.

The envelope had something round and heavy inside. And the word 'Asmodeus' written in my mother's hand on the outside. I recognized the name. A prince of hell, the demon of lust. I opened the envelope. There were two things inside. A large gold ring with a stone that looked like an eyeball with a brilliant blue iris, really kind of spiritual or mystic looking. It had "LOVE" inscribed inside it. The second item was a small slip of paper. It said, **"When your eyes watch your object, to your rhyme they will be subject."**

The ring was heavy gold and completely unelegant. I tried it on the second finger of my right hand. It was a perfect fit. Serendipity. I was admiring it on my hand when Millie stepped in. She told me the prosecutor's office said they would have something for me first thing in the morning.

I have two kinds of cases: walk-in's usually based on a news story about the Psychic PI, and Bail bond skips.

I have some open, active cases I'm working on, so I thumbed through the stack of bail skip files. I started with Haley Froeland. She had failed to appear for her court date. It was a big bail and the bail bondsman had failed to locate her for a couple of weeks so he gave me the case. I get a couple of cases a week from the local bail bondsmen. They don't advertise it, but once they run out of leads for a skip, I have better results than their folks. Once logic fails, they'll turn to a psychic. Its just business with them. They don't have a reputation to preserve.

Haley was a working girl who'd gotten fed up with her pimp. She chased him down First Avenue with a baseball bat and broke his arm and gave him a concussion. There was no doubt he deserved it, but the authorities think she should have left justice to them. She was elusive. She had a hundred working girls all over the county helping her out. Wigs, makeup, and scanty clothing were perfect disguises. No John ever looked higher than their chests. They all changed their appearances every day anyway. None of them had credit cards. The working girls had a strict cash and barter economy.

The bail bondsmen who use me know I need something their client has handled. They always get something like a paper cup, soda bottle, or a paper they handled. Ace Bail Bonds had made a $25,000 bond for her and they wanted it back. I wasn't a bond enforcement agent, so if I found her, I'd call Ace. They'd send an agent to pick her up and I'd get half the pickup fee, in this case, about $1,250.

My work was usually free of danger, but not always, so I usually took Gus with me. I opened her file, looked at her photo, and touched the paper she'd signed. Lucifer jumped into my lap and purred. I was ready. I closed my eyes and waited for a useful vision. I got something. I saw her standing on a street corner talking to a woman. Another hooker from the way they were both dressed. Dressed is a general term. Their scanty shorts and halter tops left almost nothing to the imagination.

"Gus," I called.

"He entered the office and I said, "I've got eyes on Haley Froeland. She's trolling for a john on Third and Pike. Call Ace Bail Bonds and tell them where she is. I kept my eyes closed and watched Haley. A car stopped beside the two hookers and someone talked to them through the window. It looked like the girls were both negotiating fees for their services. Haley's co-worker was the winning contractor. She got in the car and it left. Haley stayed on the corner, looking expectant, not bored. I guess all the working girls learn how to hide boredom if they want to be successful in their profession.

Success. I watched the bounty hunter walk up to Haley and take her into custody. He cuffed her and took her to a car. I opened my eyes and Lucifer said, "Ack," his congratulations for another job finished.

I made my case notes in the file, told Gus and Millie what happened, and gave Millie the info for our invoice. Time for one more.

I picked out the next file in the stack and opened it. James 'Mad Dog' Albee. Wonderful. Mad Dog was a local biker. He was a member of the "Ducks Motorcycle Club." The Ducks were a puppet club of the Outlaws in the Seattle area. They did the dirty work of the Outlaws locally. They ran an extortion ring and dealt meth to the locals. A turf war was ongoing between the Ducks and three other, smaller clubs for control of the meth business in King County. Mad Dog had been videoed stabbing a rival gang member. The victim survived and Mad Dog was charged with Aggravated Assault. The gang's lawyer had gotten him out on $50,000 bail . He told the judge Albee was a local business man, had strong ties to the community, and he was only defending himself. His case was aided because the victim had an open switchblade in his hand when police arrived.

I guess Mad Dog didn't like his chances in court, or maybe he just forgot his court date. Anyway, Alegre Bail Bonds would like him to appear. I had several pictures of Mad Dog and some grimy paperwork he signed. He should have been named pig pen like the comic strip character. In his picture, he looked like he wallowed in grease then rolled in dirt. His paperwork was filthy too. He needed a good pressure washing.

I had looked for him before. Always found him too. Useless because he was always on his hog running down a freeway. I had never been lucky enough to see an address or recognizable land mark. My only solution was to keep trying. So, here I go again. I sat in my chair and Lucifer landed in my lap. I looked at his disgusting photos, and fingered his paperwork. I always needed to wash my hands after looking for him. I closed my eyes and thought about him.

I saw him immediately. On his hog, with a gang of club members in a city. I watched and prayed and by golly, I recognized a landmark. He just rode in front of the "Hammering Man" sculpture in front of the Seattle Art Museum on First Avenue. I said, "Gus, I need you."

"Yeah, boss?"

Mad Dog is riding south on First Avenue. He just passed SAM. Get on Goggle Earth and get a street view south of there."

"OK."

"He just passed the Federal Courthouse. He's wearing a red helmet and his bike is painted red too."

"Gus, He turned into the industrial area south of the stadium. I don't see anything I recognize."

'Gus asked, "Did you see the street name? Or any business names?"

"Nope." My vision faded out. "I've lost him. What we need is a helicopter."

"Pretty pricey, boss," Gus replied.

"Thanks, Gus. He's gone." I made notes about his details and where we saw him. Next time, maybe.

I called it a day and went home.

Chapter 3

Lynn, my renter, was already there cooking something. Lynn is a wonderful roommate. I have this big old house I inherited from my mother. Four bedrooms, a parlor, a living room, a dining room, a den, an attic, and a basement. Plus a three car detached garage. All on a view lot on Queen Anne hill. Of course I pay the county $15,000 a year in property tax. If I had a mortgage as well, I'd sell the mausoleum. But I don't, so I keep it.

Lynn is my age and a gourmet cook. She's a sous chef in a fancy restaurant in Elliott Bay. I keep her rent low as long as she cooks for me. She a close friend too. I told her about the ring I'd found and she made all the appropriate sounds as I showed it to her.

"So," she said, "you have a magic love ring. Have you tried it out yet? You need to. You haven't had anyone serious since Don-."

"Wait," I yelled, "don't mention that swine's name when I'm around."

"Suzy," she said, "its been over a year now. I'll bet he's even healed by now. Besides that's our new President's name, too."

"I don't like him either, "I said "don't say that name around me, please, no matter who its referring to."

"She said, "OK, OK. Anyway, Its been a long time since you got any, Suzy. You know, 'use it or lose it, honey. So how does it work?"

We were like kids with a new toy. Excited. "So, if it works, the instructions say I have to look at my target and say a spell in a rhyme."

Lynn said, "Let's make up some rhymes and write them down, and see how it works. We'll go to a bar and try it on other people first, nothing nasty, just see if we can get people talking."

"OK, what are we rhyming?"

"Let's see," she said, "date, mate, talk, kiss, drink, even sleep?"

We made up a couple of stupid rhymes, simple things, like:

- She's first rate, ask her for a date.
- I'd like to be your mate, can I have a date?'
- She's one you don't want to miss, ask her for a kiss.'

We did several for different situations. Even some for us, just in case.

We caught the bus downtown, since neither of us wanted to worry about a car. Lucifer sat in my lap. He didn't get on with us, but after I sat down he climbed into my lap. I don't know how he does it but even if a Metro cop looks at me, he won't seem to see Lucifer. I was used to that, but it was still worrying.

Lynn knew a place near where she worked. So we soon had a booth in the Elliott Bay Brewhouse and were surveying the clientele. We picked a man and a woman. Chose rhymes appropriate for each. I looked at the man and whispered the rhyme. Then I looked at the woman and whispered her rhyme. The results were awesome. One hundred percent. If I told them to talk, they would. Even if one of them was with other people. We didn't split up couples. That wouldn't be right. We made a lot of happy people that night.

Lynn asked me to fix her up with a hunk standing and talking to some guys. So I did. He turned around and looked at Lynn and walked up to her and asked her to dance. Lynn, of course said yes and they were hanging on each other the rest of the evening. They exchanged numbers and we went home.

I was feeling a little aroused by the time we left. Maybe using the ring had an aphrodisiac effect on me? More likely it was just knowing I had helped some folks hookup for the night. I wasn't ready to try it myself. Lynn was pretty sloshed and I had a hard time getting her to the bus stop. She told me his name was Dave and he was a Seattle Cop.

Lynn dozed and I fretted on the bus ride home. I had always understood that if something was too good to be true, it usually was. The ring was pretty and seemed to be quite effective. Would there be a downside? I had read stories where magic gifts always turned around an bit you in the ass. I worried about Lynn. I worried about me for using it. How could I look up something on it? Ask an expert? Where would I find one?

I had trouble falling asleep. I worried about the ring and wondered how to find out more about things like it. I realized I was sexually aroused. I hadn't been with a man for a long time and all the thoughts of sex and the ring must have awakened that part of me. I realized I was stroking my pussy and yanked my hand away. I hadn't started that. But my arousal didn't go away. It had been months since I had even masturbated. I was very much in the mood to sit on someone's lap in cute panties. I wanted to cuddle and grind and make out a little for a couple of hours. I looked in my nightstand and Mr. Hitachi wasn't there. I remembered putting it away in my closet. I got it and plugged it I before I got back in bed. He was icy. I rubbed him around on my tummy until he warmed up. I gently rubbed the magical Mr. Hitachi up and down my slit. My arousal grew and slid into a wondrous orgasm. I put Mr. Hitachi into the nightstand, certain he was a girl's best friend.

I woke up later than usual. I felt rested and restive, like I had something important to do, but I had forgotten what. My belly was tingling and needy. Hell. I was horny again. I couldn't help it. I really wish I had someone to fuck me like the nympho I am and treat me like a princess. I wanted someone to use me like a slut and tell me I was a good girl for it. Was the Love Ring responsible for my ongoing arousal? Maybe Asmodeus liked to see women in lust.

I wrenched myself out of bed, determined to regain control of my life. No ring was going to control me. I showered and as I dried, I looked at myself in the mirror and looked again. My hair was darker. I had always had dishwater blond hair and I considered coloring it every month. Now my hair was a light auburn. There was no blond in it. I went closer to the mirror and studied my head. I think my eyes were less blue and more green, too. No, wishful thinking and self hypnosis. I had trouble finding comfortable clothes. I must have drunk too much last night. I couldn't get my bra to be comfortable. I changed it twice and all were too tight. I finally put on a sports bra that was more elastic. I finished dressings but things weren't right. My blouse and slacks were uncomfortable. I checked and there were no folds of cloth or errant socks. I looked in the mirror and my blouse was about to burst open. The space between the buttons was pulled apart. My breasts were larger, there was no way around it. And I could barely button my pants either. I looked like well endowed woman trying to squeeze into her daughter's clothes. I changed to a dressy T-shirt and pulled it over my pants. I didn't understand. I hadn't eaten more than usual for the last month. I may have to diet or buy some clothes, or both. I went down to the kitchen and found Lynn bustling around.

Lynn was ecstatic. She liked Dave and wanted to see more of him. She credited my ring with bringing him into her life. I was feeling more leery about it now. My motto is always look a gift horse in the mouth. And my second motto is anything free is worth what you paid for it. I worried I may not want to pay for it. I decided to take it off and put it back in the envelope.

I grasped it and pulled it. Nothing happened. It didn't budge. Rats. my hand must have swelled up. I looked at it and there was no way it would fit over my knuckle. It was snug around my finger. My finger would have had to be half the size it was today for it to slide on as easy as I remembered. Was it enchanted? Could my use of it have made it shrink? Now I was worried. Magic was one thing. This was personal.

Maybe it shrunk when I used it. Maybe I used it too much last night. Maybe if I didn't use it so much, it would grow again. I must have used it twenty times last night. That's it. I tired it out, used up too much magic and it got a little smaller when I emptied it. If I didn't use it so much again, it would grow. I had a feeling that trying to cut it off was not a good idea. Not an enchanted ring.

Lynn had been talking away as I pondered my problem. She stopped talking and I looked at her. She was looking at me with expectation. Oops. I asked, "What?"

Lynn asked, "When did you color your hair? It looks good."

I lied. "Yesterday, I just thought a change would be good."

"Can you go with me again tonight?"

I said, "Lynn, I'm sorry. Go where?"

She blew out an exasperated sigh and said, "OK. I'll start over. Dave asked me to meet him again at the alehouse. Can you come too? I want you to reinforce the spell so I can have a better chance of seeing him more. OK?"

I didn't want to use the ring so much. One time wouldn't hurt. And I also didn't want to disappoint my best friend. "OK, I said, what time?"

Lynn said, "Eight tonight. We'll meet him there like last time."

"All right. But I think I overused the ring last night, so I'm only going to use it a little. You come up with what you want me to say."

She pouted a little and said, "I had fun last night. Are you sure we can't use it a couple of times. We sure made some people happy with it."

"No, just once to help you and maybe once for me. I need to learn more about the ring before I use it much. And why do you want more help. It seems like you and Dave are doing fine for only one meeting. Not even a date. What do you want to do? Get him in the sack already, a first kiss, or, how about a first date?"

She looked forlorn and said, "I don't know. I've never had much luck with guys. It always starts out good then flops after a couple of dates. Maybe the magic will fix my problem."

I think she only had bad luck because all she talked about was cooking. I said, "Here's my advice. Don't talk about food or cooking. Talk about him and feed his ego. Men like that a lot. If things don't go well we can try the magic another time."

Lynn seemed to cheer up and I dashed out of the house before she had more ideas. I jumped in my car and was backing out oh the garage when I realized Lucifer was not on the passenger seat. I almost went back to get him and decided it was his fault for being slow. I was pulling into the street when he jumped over the passenger seat back and sat down. He turned his head toward me and said, "Ack!"

I think he was chastising me for making him hurry.

I parked in a garage near my office. It costs me about as much as a car payment, but its handy. I buy a monthly pass so I'll have a guaranteed spot for my car. Taking a car downtown is a hassle. But buses only work for a few miles unless you're going to a park and ride in another town. Just not what PIs need. Lucifer didn't walk with me. I saw him watching me several times as I walked from the garage to my office. Weird places like a second floor window sill. On top of a parked car. I saw his face looking out of a storm sewer grate. I even saw him looking at me from inside the display window of a hat store. I felt like he was guarding me. I don't know what a 20 pound cat could do, but I think Lucifer was more than he appeared. It made me feel warm, safe, and spooked all at once.

Gus had picked up the things of Mr. Henry from the prosecutor. Several shirts, clean underwear, some papers he'd signed for the prosecutor. A photo of him, looked like from a driver's license. He had no record, one kid in California, ex-wife in Spokane. His folks had passed. There was a job application from Boeing where he listed a brother John, living in Idaho at the time. Six years ago.

I saw something interesting. The police suspected Ralph was a white supremacist. At least he had gone to a couple of local meetings, but not a sure thing. Idaho was a center of white supremacists, neo-nazis, or Aryan Nations. Potatoe, Potahto. I wonder if Ralph leans that way?

I collected everything, got a cup of Rocket Fuel and went into my office. The first thing I saw was the white envelope with 'Asmodeus' written on it. I stuffed it in a drawer. I spread Ralph Henry's stuff out on the desk so I could see all the things at once and I closed my eyes. I felt Lucifer land in my lap.

I immediately saw a woman's face in a car. It took me a moment, but then I recognized Melanie Billings. Damn it. Old news. Forget her. After a moment her image faded. A new vision appeared.

Chapter 4

A man I didn't recognize. It wasn't Ralph Henry. My libido must have been working overtime because this man was a hunk. He looked like all my female dreams rolled into one. Tall, broad shouldered, intelligent face, narrow waist, rugged, handsome features. He was walking cautiously in a forest or jungle. He was placing his feet carefully like he was sneaking up on someone. Lots of broad leaf plants and vines. I had never seen him before. I felt a breeze and smelled salt water. And what was he doing?

Two swarthy, muscular men ran at him waving cutlasses. He lifted a hand and a broadsword appeared in it. His mouth stretched into a broad smile and he engaged them. He was magnificent. I heard the clang of their blades slamming into each other. I heard the grunts and smelled the sweat and fear of the swarthy men. I gasped at the swell of his biceps as he skimmed over the ground. It was like watching Green Bay play Roosevelt High. He was a skilled swordsman and out classed them in every way. Faster, bigger, stronger, more agile. He beat one opponent's blade aside. Faster than light his blade continued into his opponent's heart. The other enemy spun on his heel and fled. The broadsword vanished and an assault rifle appeared in his hand. He paused and turned his head like a great raptor and looked at me. His lips twisted into a knowing smile and with his free hand, threw me a kiss. He can see me! I jumped in alarm and he vanished.

I had never seen him before, but I knew him. From my imagination. This was Conan of Cimmeria. The one Robert E. Howard described in his drug induced euphoria, not the movie. This was the real thing. He was head and shoulders taller than his enemies. He had tigerish speed and incredible strength. He wielded that long broadsword like it was a bamboo stick. This was a king among men. I had lain awake after reading about the barbarian who would be a King. I had learned to masturbate to orgasm dreaming of being his Xenobia, the slave girl who he loved. I wanted to wear his chains and love him.

Everything went black and when I woke I felt fluttery and hot. I opened my eyes. What kind of vision was this? Before they were always like looking at a photograph. This one was a movie with sounds and smells. Was he real? All my other visions had been of real people. Had I started hallucinating from books? Nah. Conan never heard of a rifle. And he was wearing camouflage clothing. I felt faint and hot and realized my vagina was sopping wet and trembling. My God. I had an orgasm watching the hunk fight. I have got to stop drinking this stuff.

Lucifer normally sits in my lap while I do my visions. He was sitting on the desk in front of me and staring at my face. He was still as a statue and silent. I got the distinct impression he was worried. I couldn't help that. I was sitting in a puddle of my own juice and needed to get clean.

28

Luckily, I keep some clothes at work in case I get dirty. This was a new one. I changed and noticed my feet were sore. I had never had problems with these shoes before. I always wore simple low pumps because I often had to go into the field. The only shoes I kept at work were two and a half inch heels in case I had to go somewhere fancy. I put them on and they felt much better than the pumps. Unusual, but my body knew what it liked. I went to the bathroom to make sure I looked presentable.

I stared at the reflection in the mirror. My hair was auburn. A luxurious, dark red- brown and shimmering in the light. Fuck. What was happening to me? I saw my eyes had changed again. They were a deep emerald green. I looked like a hair coloring ad. Even my eyebrows were auburn. They were in a perfectly plucked arch highlighting the light blue eye shadow I hadn't put on. But there it was. I recognized my face, but I looked better somehow. My cheekbones were higher and the lines of my nose crisper, cleaner. I looked at myself for a long time. I liked what I saw, but didn't know how I had changed. It was scary. What else was different?

I took inventory and remembered my bra this morning. My clothes were uncomfortable. They didn't fit right. I had worn these clothes for months and they fit fine until now, My slacks were loose at the waist and too tight on my hips. My Blouse was too tight . I had always had an athletic build and uncomfortable about my boyish figure and small breasts. By all indications that was all changing overnight. My hips and breasts were getting fuller and my waist smaller. High heels were more comfortable than flats. I now had the face and hair of a starlet. The only thing I knew about that might be the cause was the ring. The Love Ring. Could my Conan be involved? I hadn't noticed most of these changes until he looked at me and blew me a kiss.

There wasn't anything I could think of to do about my looks. I mean, I looked wonderful, but I didn't know how or why. I didn't know if they would stop. I called out, "Millie, would you come to the bathroom please?"

She opened the door and looked at me in surprise. She whistled and said, "Suzanne, you look gorgeous. Your hair is wonderful. When did you change it? And you eyes. Are those contacts? And your figure. Padding? Is this a disguise? Say something, dammit."

I said, "Slow down Millie. No, its not a disguise, there's no contacts or a wig. Something happened to me last night and this morning. I don't know who or what, These changes are not my doing. It may be a ring I found yesterday, but there's no evidence. I can't explain it."

She said, "What or who is doing it, I'd like some. You look amazing. How do you feel?"

"I feel fine. Nothing hurts at all. My feet. I'm wearing my heels because the flats were uncomfortable. What ever is doing this to me thinks I look better in heels. I guess."

Millie said, "You'd better show Gus or he won't recognize you."

"Yeah, right. I raised my voice, "Gus, would you come to my office please?" Millie and I went into my office and I sat in my chair at the desk.

Gus strode in and said, "Yeah... Who... Suzy?"

I said, "Gus, I've had a makeover. What do you think?"

He said, "Suzy, you look great. I mean you looked good before but now... I wish I were even twenty years younger."

I dimpled and said, "Thank you, Gus. You should know, I didn't do any of this. Its not a disguise and there's nothing fake here. Something is changing me. I suspect its a ring I found in my desk yesterday, but I don't know for sure."

He said, "You look great. Don't take it off. You might changed back."

I went back to my office and sat back down at the desk. I was hesitant to close my eyes again. "Well," I thought, "maybe he'll come back and maybe he won't. Let me see Ralph first, please." I studied the things on my desk and handled the clothes. I closed my eyes and waited.

I'm Bret Thorne, a field wizard for MG, the Wizard's Guild. I was in the rain forests of the Philippines looking for a bad guy. A capable black magician who calls himself Sauron. HQ found his moniker on some emails the rebels exchanged. He's been helping some rebels fight the government. He whipped the soldiers pretty good before we got wind of his work. The government pulled back from the whole province. We only found out a magician was at work here by a fluke.

 Anyway, I got here this morning, but couldn't find a trace. Usually I can feel another wizard from a hundred miles away. I quartered the whole province but not a whiff. I found a rebel camp and dropped in. They started shooting at everything so I put them to sleep with a stunner. There were almost fifty guys there so I used up the charge in my stunner and put it away.

Of course, two guys I missed the first time jumped out from behind a tree and ran at me with cutlasses, of all things. I should have found a way to put them to sleep with their buddies, but I guess my blood was up so I fought them. I materialized a big broadsword and enjoyed some swordplay for the first time in years. A broadsword is too big and heavy for most people. I loved the way it looked and felt, so it was all I ever practiced with. I figured if I was good with it, I'd be good with anything lesser. These guys were enthusiastic, but not adept with their swords. I put one down and the first ran off.

I was going to zap him with a rifle when I felt someone looking at me. Not a wizard. A witch? Not a well trained one because she made no effort at concealment. Or maybe she wanted me to see her. I looked at her and saw a quite pretty young witch with rich auburn hair and a surprised look on her face. I threw her a special kiss and went after the fleeing swordsman. I decided to just put this one to sleep. He was no threat and maybe he'd know something about Sauron. When I was done here, maybe I'd look up the witch. She was quite pretty and I could track my kiss for a couple of weeks.

I searched the rebel's camp for anything that might help me find Sauron. I turned all the sleeping men face up and sent photos to HQ. One tent was larger than the rest but it was empty. I found a newspaper page laying on the ground. I folded the paper put it into a sample bag, sealed it, and sent it to the HQ forensic lab. Scant pickings for so many people, I thought.

A faint sound came to me and I extended my sense of perception outward, feeling everything. At a hundred feet or so I found a squad of rebels coming toward him. There were ten men with M-16s and they had a prisoner. A girl maybe sixteen. Her hands tied behind her, gagged with a rag and led by a length of rope tied around her neck.

'Great. Now who's the leader?' I phased into invisibility and moved next to a tree. I watched the squad until I was sure who was in charge. When they entered the camp I got out my stunner. I tripped the girl, and zapped everyone except the girl and the leader. He spun around looking for a target. I sent his rifle and pistol a mile offshore. The terrified man was about to bolt when I materialized in front of him.

I had my hands empty, palms up to show I meant no harm. I said, in Filipino, "Hello. I will not harm you. I am looking for the man who calls himself 'Sauron.' All your men are alive, just sleeping. If you tell me where to find Sauron, I will leave with the girl and not tell the government where you are. If you do not help me, you will sleep until the government takes you to prison. Will you help me?"

The man looked at Bret for a moment, then said, "Yes, I will help you."

"That is good. What is your name?"

"I am Ronick."

"You may call me Merlin. When did Sauron leave?"

"Two days ago. He just vanished."

"Did he say anything about his destination?"

"He said he was going home."

"Did he say where that was?"

"No. He only said he had a duty at home."

"Did he say if or when he would return?"

"He said he would not come back. He finished his work here ."

"What did he do here."

"He helped us take our land back from the government. He was a wizard. The army could not stand before him. With his help we drove the army out of our province. They will not soon return. Many of my men are with their families now."

"OK. Where did you get the girl?"

"Monkayo. We rescued her."

"It looks like you captured her."

"She escaped from a brothel in Monkayo. The owner caught her and was taking her back. She made so much noise we found them. He's dead and we brought her here. If she wants to stay she can. If not we'll take her to Maco. That's where her family lives. But her uncle sold her to the brothel, so maybe she won't want to go there."

I turned to the girl. "Is that true?"

She nodded her head several times.

"Will you be quiet if I remove your gag?"

She nodded again.

"OK, come here." I untied the gag and the ropes. She rubbed her wrists. "What is your name?"

"Ella."

"Ella, tell me about the place in Monkayo. Are there more girls there?"

"I do not think so, now. There were many girls locked up there, but no men came. They were going to sell us to a rich American, they said. They let me out to clean just before the buyer was due. I escaped. They caught me in an hour then these men took me away."

"Ella, think about what the place in Monkayo looked like." I watched the image form in her mind. I copied it and sent it to the tech lab at HQ with instructions to find it in Monkayo.

"Thank you, Ella. I'll find it. Where would you like to go? Do you have any relatives you would like to be with?"

"My grandmother lives in Manila. I would like to be with her, but it is a long way and I have no money."

"That's not a problem. Ronick, thank you for your help. I will not tell the government where you are. Your men will wake in an hour. Goodbye."

"Ella, do you have an address for your grandmother in Manila?"

"Yes, 149 Chartereusse Street, 1718 Paranaque City, Metro Manila."

I sent it to HQ and they gave me coordinates.

"Ready, Ella?"

"Yes, senor, do you have a car?"

"Close your eyes, Ella." I put her asleep and caught her.

I teleported us to the address she gave me and woke her.

"Senor, how?"

"You fell asleep and missed the fun part, Ella. Take me to your grandmother's place.

She led me up a flight of stairs and knocked on a door. Her grandmother opened the door and they fell into each others arms. I gave the grandmother the cash I had on me. I always carry a lot when I'm on assignment, so they could live on it for a few years. I went back to HQ to see what they had found out if anything, from what I sent them.

They had found the building in Monkayo. I took a couple of soldiers with me and went there. It was empty but there was evidence that many girls had been kept here. I looked with my second sight and saw a few tendrils of spells laying about. Probably a sleeping spell from the feel of the tendrils. I could also tell who they came from. It was familiar, "Bart, what are you up to?" I thought.

Chapter 5

It worked this time. I saw Ralph. He was sitting at a picnic table with trees behind him. There were three other men sitting at the table. Everyone was wearing a long sleeve shirt. Two of the men had vests. All had hats. Looked outdoorsy to me. Idaho was feeling good, right now.

Who the heck was the hunk? Why was he in my vision? Why did I get all my senses activated? Was it a dream or a vision? Maybe I was getting hallucinations or day dreams in my vision pattern? Was he responsible for some or all of my changes? Was I changing to the Psychotic PI?

OK. Back to the real world. I called a friend at the King County Sheriff's Department. I told him I was working a case for the county prosecutor and asked him to check out John Henry in Idaho. He called back in a few minutes. John was known to the Idaho cops. He lived outside of Bonners Ferry in Idaho's panhandle. About twenty miles from the Canadian Border. He'd had a few encounters but never convicted of anything but traffic infractions.

I wasn't about to go scrambling through the Idaho forests looking for Ralph. I needed him to come to me. I had his email address. I didn't know if he checked it often, but it cost nothing to try. I wrote,

'Dear Mr. Ralph Henry. Congratulations, you have been selected at random to receive our grand prize.

The Washington Ford Dealer's Association is celebrating our one hundredth year. You will receive a brand new Ford F-150 4x4 XLT Pickup. You can pick up the prize in either Seattle, Spokane, Vancouver, or Bellingham. Please contact us within seven days to claim your prize . If you do not wish to accept this prize, do not reply and we will select another winner.

Sincerely, Suzanne Ryder, Customer Relations Manager'

Now, we'll see if greed conquers caution.

I went to the Alehouse with Lynn and Lucifer. Cats aren't allowed on a bus or in a restaurant. Lucifer had way of not being noticed when he didn't want to be. Think Cheshire cat in Alice in Wonderland. I could always find him if I wanted to, but he was a master of disguise and tiny places. We saw Dave with his buddies as soon as we walked in. Lynn pulled me into the ladies room and gave me her rhyme. I was to wait until Dave was looking at Lynn then repeat the rhyme. It went, "Love is blind, you can't get Lynn out of your mind." Cheesy, right? The ring doesn't seem to have a bit of class.

"Lynn," I reminded her, "Only talk about him. If he asks about you, only say you're a chef, talk about him, only him. No food. Not what you like. Only him. He is the only interesting thing in your life. Make him think he is the strongest, bravest, smartest cop in Seattle."

We went into the bar and Lynn called to Dave. He looked at her, I looked at him and repeated the rhyme. It seemed to work. Dave left his buddies and sat with Lynn at a table for two. I studied the ring. It didn't get any tighter when I used it, so that was a relief.

I found myself being studied by every single male in the place. The changes in my looks had apparently made me quite attractive to men. I guess women too. I was hit on by four men and two women. I finally asked one guy to sit and talk to me just to stop the line of suitors. We told each other outrageous lies about ourselves and our jobs. I used the ring just a little to convince him to stay and just talk while I surveyed the room.

I looked around and found some people eying each other from afar. It would have been easy to use the ring to get them together. But I was still a little afraid of overusing it so I tried the direct approach. I asked my new friend to wait and went to the woman. I said, "Hi, I'm Suzy Ryder, and the guy at the fourth table over wants to meet you. Would you like that?

She looked me up and down and asked, "Why do you care?"

So I lied, "I lost a bet and now I've got to try to find two strangers and get them to talk. Look him over and if you want to meet him, tell me your name. I'll introduce you. If you don't hit it off., just tell him you're not interested and he'll leave."

She said, "A bet. OK, he looks cute. I'm Jill."

"Shiny. I'll go talk to him. Maybe I'll bring him back."

I walked to the guy who'd been watching my conversation with Jill. I said, "Hi, I'm Suzy and the lady I was talking to is Jill. She would like to meet you, if you're OK with that?"

He studied me and said, "Hi Suzy. I saw you talking to her. You don't know her do you?"

"Nope, like I told her, I lost a bet and I have to get two strangers to talk to each other. I saw you and her exchanging looks, so I thought you two needed an introduction. If you'd like to meet her, tell me your name and I'll introduce you. If not, I'll just leave you alone."

He looked at me, then at her. He said, "OK, I'm game. My name is Jim."

"OK, come on, let's go meet her."

He stood up, I took his arm and we walked to Jill. "Jill, meet Jim, Jim, meet Jill." I pulled out a chair across from Jill and left. I went back to my seat and watched them for a while. They each had a drink and I looked for someone I'd like to meet.

I thought up a safe rhyme: "If you don't have a partner and you think I'm cute, come buy me a drink and don't be mute." I looked for someone I'd like to meet. I also thought up one to get rid of them if it didn't work out: 'I'm sorry, but this is moot, so you need to scoot.' I sent my new friend away and watched the room.

Soon, a threesome came in, One girl, two guys and both guys looked good. I watched to see who the girl was with. Once I was sure, I aimed my rhyme at the free one and released the ring. He looked around, found me, said goodbye to his friends and came over. The ring didn't dawdle around.

His name was Allen and he was a computer geek at Microsoft. That meant he was well off and educated. I felt safe with the ring to do my heavy lifting for me. We got on well and I wanted to see how he was in bed. I told Lynn I was going home with Allen and not to make too much noise when she came in. He took me home. He drove a BMW, so he had good taste in cars, anyway. Lucifer rode in the backseat. I don't think Allen twigged to him. I told him I couldn't invite a man I hadn't even kissed into my home. He took care of that formality without hesitation. He was a good kisser. He made me feel like I was the center of his universe in one long, memorable kiss. So I let him into my lair. I felt like a lioness ready to spring. I led him to my bedroom and we got in bed. His foreplay was good, but he was finished before I was done. Unsatisfying. I sent him home without a kiss and threw his number away. He was all about gratifying himself and didn't have a clue about me. Men!

I sat on the porch and ate a pint of rocky road after he left. I noticed the ring was no tighter. Good. I'd be more specific in my next rhyme. I had a grand view looking over downtown lights and across the Sound to Bainbridge Island. I was feeling a little sad. I had no one in my life. Lucifer nudged my hand with his head. I petted him and said, "You're always here for me, aren't you?"

I had a magic ring to find love. Yet all I wanted was Conan. The modern one. The one in my vision. Was he real? Could he be real? Did I have a chance of finding my dream man? I wondered how I could do that? Was it as simple as closing my eyes and trying to see him again? Talk to him? I know he saw me. What if he was a bad guy? No. I didn't believe that.

Then I went back to bed and my old friend, Mr. Hitachi. At least appliances are dependable.

I lay there, waiting for sleep to claim me and wrote rhymes for tomorrow. I'm ashamed to say the best I came up with was: "If you don't have a partner and won't come before I'm done, buy me a drink and stroke my bum."

When I thought of this disaster, I got a picture of my Conan vision rubbing my ass. I bet he wouldn't go off too soon. It was a grand way to fall asleep.

Chapter 6

I woke up sweating and horny. I had the image of my mystery man in my mind. I wanted him, not the feeble mass of humanity that peopled my city. I didn't even want Mr. Hitachi now. I went to the gym above my office at 6 am the next morning. I needed to work up a sweat and get the mystery man out of my head so I could work. Lucifer watched me exercise from atop an abs machine. There were some good looking young men working out. They saw me and came over to talk, but I couldn't work up any interest. They were fit and would have attracted my interest a few days ago. Now they seemed pallid, insipid, and uninteresting.

I had heard magic often worked like this. I could inspire any of these men to love but I didn't want them. The one I wanted wasn't here. Even if he were, I doubt magic would work on him. He was like an elemental, fire, water, air, wind. Not to be tamed by anyone but a god. I gave up on exercise and showered. Lucifer brought me a towel when I was done. After I was dressed I realized I was still obsessing on my mystery man. I needed to get to work and think of something else.

Millie was glad to see me. "Well, where have you been? Out partying with your new look? You didn't answer your phone and Lynn said you left early this morning. I've been looking everywhere. You have a new client. I've been stalling him for almost an hour."

"Sorry, Millie. I went to the gym. I didn't have anything scheduled so..."

"Ms. Ryder, this is a business. New business walks in the door. If I knew where you were..."

"Yes, you're quite right, Millie. My bad. I'm sorry. I'll let you know in the future when I'm going to be late. Tell me about the client."

She said, "Mr. James Carstairs. He has a champion race horse. It was stolen last night. He's in your office."

I got a cup of my rocket fuel and went in my office.

Mr. Carstairs was a florid man of fifty or so with a large belly. He was not in a good mood.

I said, "Good morning Mr. Carstairs. I understand your horse was stolen."

"Yes, yes. Last night. He was gone this morning without a trace. I need you to find him. I will pay a bonus if you can find him in less than a week." He handed me a picture of a tall black horse.

I took it and studied it. "Big. Why is a week important?"

"I sold him yesterday and I'm to deliver him in a week."

"I see. Well, I need something of the horse's. A blanket, tack, horseshoe, something that's touched him."

"I understood that from the newspaper stories," he said. He opened a case and handed me a bit. "This is Magellan's"

"Cool name. I take it he's fast."

"That's an understatement."

"Mr. Carstairs, understand, its my job to find him. The police will take care of the thieves and you will have to take care of transporting him. I'm not equipped for that. My fee is $2,000, in advance, for looking for him."

He said, "OK. I'll double that if you find him in a week."

OK. Millie will prepare an engagement contract and if you'll sign it and give her the $2,000, I'll get to work." I opened the door and said, "Millie, Mr. Carstairs has agreed to sign an engagement contract. $2,000 for the engagement and a $2,000 bonus if I find his horse, Magellan, in less than a week. Goodbye, Mr. Carstairs. Make sure Millie has your contact information."

I sat down at my desk. Lucifer jumped up and sniffed the bit. He turned up his nose and sat in my lap. I put my hand on the bit, leaned back and closed my eyes. As usual, I saw the horse. Inside a horse trailer motoring down a highway. The trailer had a window. It gave me a tiny view of the outside world. It was all I had, so I watched the window. It paid off I saw an Interstate 90 sign. I called Millie.

"Yeah," she said. I didn't open my eyes.

"Millie, the stolen horse, Magellan, is in a horse trailer heading east on I-90. By now he's probably in Idaho. Get a map up on my computer and I'll see if I can spot anything to pinpoint his location. I'm looking out a small window in the horse trailer."

"Ms. Ryder, you are spooky."

"Once you get it up, call Gus and see if he can do the map for me so you can watch the front.."

"OK," she said.

After a while I said, "Hey, he just passed a turn for US 2 but they didn't take it. Where's US 2 and I-90?"

Gus said, "Spokane. Its only 20 miles from the Idaho border."

"Call the State Patrol. Tell them there's a horse trailer with a stolen horse on I-90 east of US 2, traveling east. Call the Idaho State Patrol too."

"OK," said Gus.

I heard him calling. In a minute he said, "They want to know how you know this."

I said, "Tell them I have a GPS tracker on the horse."

My vision cut off. Just like that. It went away. Its never gone away before. I opened my eyes. I said, "Tell them my tracker just went dead."

Gus asked, "What?"

"My vision stopped. Tell them my tracker went dead."

Gus said, "They checked the road from the air. No horse trailer."

"Well, that sucks," I said. OK. Go back to work. I'll pick this up later. I'll check on Ralph." I put the bit and picture in a box labeled 'Magellan' and put it in a filing cabinet drawer. I got out the one labeled "Ralph Henry," and took out some clothes. I held one in each hand and closed my eyes. Lucifer plopped back into my lap. I got a vision, but it was all black, like he was in a dark room. No light at all. Oh, well. I'll have to wait.

I put Ralph's things away and looked at my email to see if he'd responded. Yes, he did. He said he would be happy to meet me at the dealer in Spokane. the day after tomorrow. I replied that I'd be there and suggested we meet at eleven am at Wendle Ford. I texted the prosecutor. I told him I had located Ralph Henry and he'd meet me in Spokane at Wendle Ford at eleven am day after tomorrow.

I heard the office phone ring and Millie answer it. The intercom buzzed and Millie told me it was Dave Sherry from the prosecutor's office. I picked it up said hello and Dave said, "Great job Suzanne. Do you want to ride over with us to pick him up?"

"No thanks. I've got another case that seems to be in that neck of the woods. I'll go over with Gus and after you get Ralph, we'll go on to Idaho."

"OK. meet you at the Ford dealer at 10?"

"Suits. See you there, Dave."

I hung up and told Millie and Gus about the Spokane trip.

I opened my file drawers and looked through a couple of old cases that hadn't gone anywhere. I had a stolen diamond that had been in a dark place for more than a year. The insurance company wanted me to check on it periodically. I had a stolen car that I could see was stored on blocks in a garage somewhere. My favorite was a stolen motorcycle currently being ridden in China.

I heard a commotion in the outer office and stuck my head out. Gus and Millie were standing in front of a priest, a nun, and a bloodhound, who was drooling on the floor. Gus was arguing with the priest, while Millie and the nun watched.

I heard the priest say, "I must search these premises for the demon. He must be exorcised before he takes another soul."

Gus said, I haven't seen anyone new here. What does he look like? Twelve feet tall and horns? Bright red? Pitchfork?"

"You jest at your peril. He can take any form he desires."

"Well, how can you tell if you've found him," asked Gus?

The priest said, "I have a demon sensor. This," he pointed to the bloodhound, " is Horus and he can sense demons."

"Riiight," said Gus.

The priest said, indignantly, "Stand aside my good man. This is for the good of humanity. I must find him before he harvests more souls."

Gus folded his arms and said nothing.

I decided I should help. My office after all. I walked out and stood beside Gus. "Good morning, I'm Suzanne Ryder and this is my office. I'm a Private Investigator. Who are you?"

The priest said, "I'm Father Magnus. I've been charged with locating and exorcising a demon currently in Seattle."

"Father Magnus," I asked, "why do you think he might be here?"

He pointed to the bloodhound and said, "This is Horus. He 's trained to detect demons and he gave an indication of demon activity at your door."

I looked down and Horus was licking my foot. I asked, "Is this how he indicates demon activity?"

Father Magnus looked down and said, "Horus, stop that." He pulled the dog back a few feet, and said, "Sister, would you mind?"

The nun behind Magnus hurried forward, dropped to her knees in front of me. She took a handkerchief from her pocket, and began wiping my shoe.

I stepped back and said, "Stop that. Stand up. Who are you?"

Father Magnus said, "I beg your pardon, this is Sister John Hancock. She has taken a vow of silence."

She stood up and scurried back behind Father Magnus.

I asked, "Father, how do you know there is a demon in Seattle?"

He said, "My order is responsible for protecting the world from the demons. We watch them closely. Two days ago I received a notice that the demon Asmodeus was in Seattle and ordered to remove him. Horus has been with me for years and is quite reliable. Since he doesn't feel a demon now, he must have moved on. I'm sorry to have bothered you."

Asmodeus! My heart froze as I recalled seeing that name on my mother's envelope. Was he somehow associated with the ring? The one I couldn't get off?

The one that made people subject? Oh damn, damn, damn.

"Asmodeus," I asked?

Father Magnus said, "Yes, the demon of lust. He lures people with the pleasures of the body, greed and gambling. I've been looking for him in every cabaret, strip club, gym, casino, race track, bingo parlor, and high school in the city."

"High school," I asked?

"He said, "Oh yes, adolescent hormones and undeveloped frontal lobes, you know. Some of the worst lust I see."

"Father," I asked, "do demons do things to objects as well as people? Could this demon leave like a calling card, you know, curse my building or my door or something?"

He said, "Well, its rare. They usually try to work directly on a person. One theory is that they have to affect a person in order to get the soul. But Beliat seems to have cursed the Ferry Tacoma. Don't understand that."

"OK," I said. No demons here. Try the gym upstairs. There's always a lot of lust up there."

PART 2 : Magic

Chapter 7

Magnus and his minions left and I told Gus, "Next time a wierdo comes in, see if they have money to hire me." I went back to my office.

I brooded over the ring and demons. I got online and looked up everything I could on demons, Asmodeus, and witches. I found a couple of women who claimed to be witches. I talked to them and they were into the occult and paganism. I couldn't find anyone who actually cast spells or enchanted objects. If there were practicing witches and wizards out there, they were not advertising themselves. I spent all afternoon on my research and all I got was a headache.

I popped a couple of Aleve and went up to the gym to exercise. Sweat was good for relaxing my mind. I worked out for an hour and got sweaty. I relaxed in the hot tub until I was wrinkled and limp. Lucifer sat on a towel and regarded me. He did not understand my need to immerse myself in water periodically. I was drying out on a recliner and made the tactical error of closing my eyes, just for a moment.

I leaned back and closed my eyes. I remembered his face, his smile, his kiss. And there he was. He was sitting down and reading something. He looked at me and spoke. His voice was low and friendly. He said, "Hello again. I'm Bret Thorne."

I spoke aloud and said, hello, Bret Thorne, I'm Suzanne Ryder."

He said, "Hold on, I'll come to you." He vanished from my vision. I opened my eyes and he was standing in front of me, still smiling. Lucifer wandered over, interested but still aloof. He sniffed at Bret while we talked.

I nearly jumped out of my skin. "Where did you come from?"

"Manila."

"Right. Of course. How did you do that?"

"Teleportation? Its really handy. No lines, no crowding, no busybodies bothering you. And it has door to door service."

"Well," I said, "I can see that. How do you do it?"

He said, "I can't explain the details yet. You don't have the vocabulary. You can probably learn if you want. You're a witch so you have the talent. You just need some training."

"I'm not a witch, I don't think. I'm a psychic."

"Then you're a witch, you just haven't been to school. Was your mother or father a witch?"

"Mother, I think. She wouldn't talk about it."

"Yeah. That happens sometimes. You're pretty. Why did you call me?"

I felt the heat rising in my face, dammit. "Thank you. I didn't know I was. I mean, I saw you earlier today and my thing is visions and there you were. I was wondering if you were real or a hallucination. So I sat here and closed my eyes and thought about you."

"Yeah, OK. That's called 'calling me' in wizard talk. And that's how I know you're a witch. Non-witches use a telephone."

"Wow. You're a wizard? That's so cool."

"Its not all fun and games."

"What do you do. I mean as a wizard."

"I'm a field operative. Most of the time I find black magicians and neutralize them."

"You kill black magicians."

"Usually I just take away their powers. Not everyone born with special abilities plays nice with others."

Bang! The door to the hot tub room flew open and Horus was bounding toward us baying like a hell hound.

Father Magnus was standing in the doorway yelling, "That must be him. Don't let him escape." I saw Sister John Hancock behind Father Magnus, peering around his arm at us.

Bret grabbed my arm and we were sitting in his car. It said Porsche on the gear shift knob. He started the car and we drove sedately away. He asked, "Friends of yours?"

"Nope. He was in earlier looking for Asmodeus. He got word the demon was in Seattle and its his job to exorcise him."

"What's with the dog? Rabid?"

"No. Father Magnus said his name is Horus and he's a demon sensor. Kind of like the drug-sniffing dogs. He sniffs demons."

"He needs more training. There's a big difference between demons and wizards or witches."

"Maybe he can just tell the difference between humans and others."

The traffic stopped. Rush hour in Seattle, as always. Bret turned into a parking garage. Then we were stopped on a bluff looking over the lights of Seattle, across Puget Sound. I asked, "Where.."

"Bainbridge Island," he said. "I wasn't going anywhere particular and the view is nice here."

We were both quiet for a while, just looking out across the Sound. I put my hand on his and looked at him. He was sort of magnificent. I askcd, "Would you tell me about magic and why you hunt black magicians?"

"There's not a lot to tell about magic. You've seen some of the Star Wars flicks?"

"Of course."

"Well its kind of like 'The Force.' Its all around us. Only a few people can use it. and the ability is inherited. We haven't been able to show anyone without the family history how to use it. Its kind of like a muscle too. The more you use it, the stronger you become in it. There's a lot of training we've developed that works on specific 'muscles,' if you will. I'm a combat wizard. I've worked hard to learn how to fight black magicians. They can be nasty to fight because a lot of them aren't entirely sane."

"So, I can improve my use of magic?"

"Sure. You need some training and practice."

"Is there a school or something?"

My organization runs a school, of course. I don't know of any others, but I can ask. If you sign up with my organization, they'll train you. But you have to work for them too."

"I have a business now. Could I be kind of a reserve officer, like the police have?"

"Oh, yeah. We have quite a lot of those. They're mainly spotters for us."

"OK. Enough work talk. Would you take me to my place? I want to change out of my swim suit."

"OK, what's the address? And I like your swim suit."

I told him and poof, we were parked in my driveway. We went up on my porch and sat on the couch.

He said, "This is a nice place. Yours?"

"Yep, all mine."

"I think I'd like a nice place like this sometime. I move around too much now to enjoy it. From the big house and the view, I guess you inherited money or have a good job."

"None of the above. I'm a working stiff and my take home barely covers the taxes on the place. I inherited it when my mom passed."

"I see you've got a leak in the roof and a little dry rot. I'll fix it for you."

"Thanks, but I just wanted to meet you, not put you to work."

"Its my pleasure. and its no bother. There. Its done."

"Come on. You didn't move."

"Didn't have to. Wizard."

"Right. So what did you do?"

"Wizards can change objects. I fixed the wood, added more waterproof material and replaced the broken tiles. I looked like something hard hit it. Maybe a tree branch? Its no harder than just thinking about it once you learn how. You saw me make a sword and a gun the first time, right?"

"Yeah, I did, OK, but how did you know it was leaking?"

"Wizards also have a strong sense of perception. I can sense everything around me, its a sense you can develop. In this case, something just didn't feel right, so I dug a little deeper and saw the problem."

"That is so cool. But, you could put all the home repair folks out of work."

"I'm usually too busy with the bad guys to find roof leaks. Say, I'm starving. I haven't eaten all day would you like to go grab a bite?"

Would I ever. He looked good enough to eat, but I guess food would do for now. "Sounds good. Do you know anywhere in Seattle?"

Chapter 8

He smirked at me. "Teleport, remember. Do you like seafood? "

"Love it."

"OK. Close your eyes."

I did and felt warm sunshine.

"OK, Open your eyes."

We were standing on a boardwalk next to a white sand beach in dazzling sunshine. I was wearing a bikini and a wrap. He was in shorts and silk shirt. We were standing in front of shops and restaurants.

"Where are we," I asked?"

"Barcelona. Maximilio's has the best seafood on the whole Mediterranean."

"Bret," I said, "you're showing off. But its so cool."

"Suzy, I don't often have the chance to impress a beautiful lady. I rarely get to just enjoy my powers by doing something nice for people. Indulge me."

"OK, for now. Excuse me for a moment. "I visited the ladies room and was even more surprised by my reflection in the mirror. My cheap earrings had been replaced by gold studs with diamonds. My hair was cut, styled and shinier than I remembered. It was kind of neat having a wizard around.

When I went back to the table I said, "You gave me a makeover on the way here, I see."

"Like it?"

"Yes, a lot. Did you go to beauty school too?"

"Nope. I just pictured you in my mind."

"And this is what you thought I should look like?"

I should tell you that my imagination is fucking you like crazy right now, but that would be crude. "No, My first image was of you naked, but then I came to my senses and thought how you would like to look."

I smiled. "Play your cards right big boy and you might get your wish."

He ordered us a big tureen of bouillabaisse and heavenly bread. Why can't I find bread like this in Seattle? I had a glass of burgundy. It was all delicious. When we finished it was still midday in Barcelona. Bret said, "Its about 8 pm in Seattle. Do you want to go home or would you like to walk around Barcelona for a little while. You know, just see the sights?"

I was like a little girl again, "Oh, can we sightsee? Please. I've never been anywhere outside the US."

"See the sights, my pleasure." He bought a tourist map from a kiosk and said, "We don't have all day if you're going to get any sleep tonight. So I'm going to be your tour guide but I only can tell you what's in this map about the places. We can come back in the future. No airfare or passport needed."

"I'm sure you will be an excellent guide. Lead on, Bret."

He opened the map and I took his arm.

A flicker and we were standing in front of the Sagrada Familia, a Gaudi designed church. It was fantastic and worth the trip to Barcelona just to see it. It looked like Disney commissioned Escher to design something with lots of towers. We bounced around Barcelona never staying in one place more than ten minutes. Teleportation is the only was to see the sights of a city. After a couple of hours of seeing Barcelona, what I remember the most is Gaudi. He seemed to have put his imprimatur on the whole city.

He saw me yawn and was contrite, "I'm sorry, you must be exhausted. Its almost 10 pm in Seattle. Let's take you home."

I raised my hand to stifle another yawn and lowered my hand in the Seattle darkness. I could get used to this. We were standing on my porch and Lucifer yowled at me from a chair. I had forgotten him. It was the first time I had been away from him in years. He was not happy. Bret squatted in front of him and said, "I'm sorry. I didn't know."

Lucifer said, "Ack, meow."

Bret said, "Yes, we'll take you along when we do this again. I promise."

I asked, "Are you talking to him?"

Bret stood up and replied, "Yes. I didn't know you had a familiar."

I said, "I didn't either. Lucifer has been my cat ever since my mother died. I can't leave him behind. He's always there. I think he's magical."

Bret said, He told me he's your familiar. You know he watches out for you. Familiars are the least understood form of sentient life we know of. We suspect they aren't from this universe. They seem to have a different relationship to time and space than ours. He was quite upset when he couldn't find you. He takes his job protecting you seriously. I apologized and promised not to separate you two in the future."

"You spoke English," I said accusingly.

"Yes, he understands English but can't speak it. Wrong vocal setup. At least in this form. You know he's a shape-shifter?"

I looked at Lucifer and said, "I've suspected it, but never caught him at it."

Bret said, "I expect he doesn't change often. Its a lot of work. Different mass in each form, you know. Anyway, I think he's calmed down now."

I was wide awake and aroused. I walked over to Bret and stood in front of him, quite close and smiled up at him. "Thank you for a wonderful day . Would you come in for a moment? I want to get to know you much better."

He said, "Are you sure. Its been a long day and you should sleep."

"Bret Thorne, I've never been more sure of anything in my life. If you don't come in, I won't sleep a wink all night." I took his hand in mine and led him in the door. Lynn was nowhere in sight. Good.

"Would you like something to drink?"

He said, "I'm in the mood for some Drambuie, I think."

I started to say I didn't have any when I saw the open bottle and two small liqueur glasses on the coffee table. I said, I think I would like that, too." I sat beside him on the couch and he poured the amber fluid into the two glasses. He handed me one and lifted his in toast. He said, "May you look back fifty years from now and agree that today was the worst day of your life."

I lifted my glass and said, "Amen." We each took a sip and I savored the warm, burn of the liqueur in my mouth. I put my glass down and took his from him and put it on the table. I climbed into his lap and kissed him, long and hard. Our tongues danced the lover's gavotte. I had never been happier. I put my arms around his neck and I felt his go around me and pull me close.

When we broke for air, I whispered in his ear, "Sir, I fear you have stolen my heart. Are you ready to take my body, too?"

He stood up still holding me and said, "My lady, I would treasure the opportunity to give you pleasure. Would you like to retire to your bedroom, or would you like another taste of magic?"

My mind whirled at the thought of making love in a magical setting. Then I thought, No, let's savor ourselves in the dark. I won't be looking at anything other than him. I said, "My bedroom is perfect."

He carried me up the stairs as if I were weightless. He stood me in the bedroom and turned me to face him. My eyes weren't as high as his shoulder. I'm 5'10" ,so he must be almost 6'5" tall. He was twice as wide as me and had large muscles. He could throw me across the room if he wanted. Instead he picked me up and kissed me. I was engulfed in his arms and dwarfed by his assurance and presence. He was tremendous in every way imaginable. He handed me something in black lace and said, "Put this on, please."

I opened it up. It was a sleeping mask. I put it over my head and everything went black. I felt my clothes slide down my body. His bare skin touched mine and I burned all over. I felt the heat radiating from my belly. I must be glowing, I'm so hot.

He said, "Just feel." He picked me up like I was weightless. He lay me on my back on the bed and said, "Lift your knees and place your feet tight against your bottom."

"Spread your knees wide. Put your hands behind your head. Don't move."

He sat on the bed beside me and played with my breasts . He kneaded them and rolled my nipples between his fingers. He was gentle, but as my nipples hardened , they were right on the edge of pain. He took one hand to my loins and started stroking my labia. They swelled instantly and soon were spreading themselves in invitation. He stroked my inner lips and I was soon panting my need. My belly spasmed over and over and my love juices flowed into my needy lips.

"Bret, Sir, please take me. I need you in me. Please take me, I beg you."

He stroked my pussy, lightly with his huge hand. I climaxed as soon as his hand touched me. I bucked and screamed, "YES. Oh yes." I moaned my pleasure and he kept rubbing, stimulating me. I was so helpless in his grip. I couldn't move any way except to spasm and buck in my passion. I was a tightly coiled ball of heat rapidly growing hotter. His hands were merciless and so incredibly effective.

I climaxed again. I was lost in my heat. I had no control. He was a master playing me like an instrument. I squealed, I pled, I writhed under his hands. I couldn't stop climaxing. Finally, he climbed on me and we merged. I was wonderfully stretched and filled. He pumped a few times, each one driving me higher until we came together. His hot sperm flooding into me in the greatest ecstasy I had ever known. I screamed with joy and love and fainted.

I lay in bed with his arms around me. He was wonderful and he didn't go off too soon. I had at least three orgasms before he had one. He was a master lover and knew just how to play my body for maximum pleasure. I would remember this night for a long time. I had never lived with a man but I thought this one would be fine to live with.

Before we had sex I was powerful. I made the decision to let him enter me. I wanted him so bad. Now that we had made love, he had the power. He could decide to love me again or leave. I had submitted to him and given him my power. The only way I would ever have power over him would be if he decided to stay faithful to me. Since I wanted him, my only goal now was to do whatever it took to keep him faithful. My choices were limited to those that pleased him. OK, that was what I wanted to do anyway.

Chapter 9

I awoke in the morning alone in bed and felt a loss. I wanted him beside me. Heck, I was ready for another lesson in love. As I thought "Love" the ring came to mind. I wondered if Bret would know about such things. I smelled breakfast smells. I got a robe on and went downstairs. Bret was sitting at the kitchen table and there were two covered platters on the table.

I walked over to him and kissed him then said, "Good morning."

He stood up and kissed me properly. When I opened my eyes again my robe was gone. How did he do that?

Bret said, "Morning beautiful. You shouldn't greet me like that or I'll have to send the food away and take you back to bed. You taste better than the food."

I said, "Let me eat first. I'm hungry."

"Good idea, you'll need your energy. Would you like some eggs for breakfast?"

"Sure, do you have a chef standing by?"

"Better. How do you like them? Is two OK?"

"Over medium, please and two is great."

He lifted a cover and pulled out a plate. Two eggs over medium, four pieces of bacon, crisp hash browns and an orange slice.

I said, "Thank you. How did you know what I wanted?"

"Magic," he said. He took out a plate for himself with three eggs.

After a couple of bites I asked, "Bret, I have a ring my mother left. I found it in an envelope inside my desk. She had written on the envelope "Asmodeus." The ring has the word "LOVE" inscribed inside it. There was a slip of paper in the envelope that said, "When your eyes watch your object, to your rhyme they will be subject."

He eyed me and asked, "Did it work?"

"How do you know I used it?"

"Honey," he said, "you're a beautiful, young woman and a witch. Of course you tried it. So, did it work?"

I sighed, "Yes, it worked fine. But now it shrunk and I can't get it off. Yesterday a priest came to my office looking for Asmodeus. He thought Asmodeus was nearby."

"Would you show it to me?"

I held up my hand, stared at it and he felt it with his fingers. He said, "Asmodeus is not inhabiting it now. The ring is enchanted. I don't feel anything harmful in it. I might be able to remove the spell. I'm not sure because I don't know all the elements of the spell. I know a specialist back at HQ that would know more about it. Would you like to see her?"

"I thought a moment. "Yes," I said, "I would like to be sure this is safe."

"OK, let me check on her schedule. He was quiet a moment and said, "Sorry, she is out on an assignment. She should be back in a few days. I'll take you there then. In the meantime, you should probably avoid using it."

"OK. Can I ask you about something else?"

"Shoot."

"I told you I use visions to locate things and people. Yesterday I had a problem, a vision was working fine when it just stopped."

He asked, you mean it ended or it froze?"

"It ended. My vision just went away like turning off a light.

"Well, two possibilities occur to me. First, your mind ended it because you were tired or distracted. How long had you been watching this vision?"

"It was a long time, more than an hour."

The second possibility is that a wizard or witch detected you and blocked your vision."

"What, someone can do that?"

"Sure. Any trained wizard or witch can block a sight. Its the only way we can keep any privacy. If you want, I can ride along with you on this vision and see if a wizard is blocking you."

"What do you mean, 'ride along.'"

You just start your vision and I'll watch. You won't know I'm there unless I step in."

I asked, "Can we try it now?"

"Sure," he said, do it now and I'll go along."

Lucifer jumped into my lap. I didn't have Magellan's bit with me, but it wasn't always necessary for second or third visions. I closed my eyes and thought about Magellan. I saw him. He was in a sunny pasture. I could see mountains behind him. I rotated my viewpoint and saw a red barn and a blue pickup. I couldn't see the license plate. It was sideways to me. I always see the object of my vision in my field of view, but I can move around it. I moved away from Magellan, trying to get far enough back to see the truck's license plate. Suddenly I felt a fierce pain in my head. I screamed and it was gone. I opened my eyes and saw Bret's serious face.

I asked, "What happened?"

He said, "You were attacked by a wizard. Not a powerful one, probably half trained. He won't be trying that again. I blocked his attack as soon as it started and I zapped him, hard. I didn't pull my punch so he could be dead now. I got a location from him too, so I know where your horse is now. Want me to bring it back?"

My head still ached and I said, "Yes, please. Just put him in the back yard and I'll contact his owner."

Bret said, OK. He's here now. You should know that when you use your visions to look at a wizard, they can see you and know your location. It makes you vulnerable to attack. This one won't be a problem for you. I zapped him before he could get your location. That's why I think he wasn't fully trained. The horse was in Idaho. Stay away from there if possible. If not, I should help you."

"I have another case I'm doing for the county prosecutor. One of their witnesses may be in Idaho. I am supposed to meet the guy in Spokane tomorrow morning and the police will pick him up."

""Suzy, have you used your visions to look at this guy?"

"Yes, and they seem to work OK on him. I saw him yesterday morning sitting at a picnic table with some guys dressed warmly. Since then I've only seen darkness, like he's asleep in a dark room. I set a lure for him via email and he took the bait and agreed to meet me at Wendle Ford in Spokane tomorrow at 11 am."

Bret said, "I'm getting a bad feeling. Would you call up your vision of the guy you're looking for?" I'll be with you, even closer, so no attack will come through."

This was the last thing I wanted to do, but I trusted Bret. I closed my eyes and thought of Ralph Henry. It came immediately. Again, just an inky blackness.

Bret said, "OK. Stop."

I opened my eyes.

He said, "Don't bother going tomorrow. That guy is dead and in a coffin. He didn't agree to meet you. Call off the police. They're out of their league. Why did you think he was in Idaho?"

"His brother is a white supremacist that lives in Idaho, up in the panhandle, near Canada. I thought Ralph might have gone there. Can you get his body. I won't get paid unless I can produce him. Can you put the coffin and his body in my garage?"

Bret looked at me. and said, "Suzy, not only are you beautiful and gutsy and great in bed, but you're not a bit squeamish. I think I'm in love. OK, he was in Northern Idaho, near Bonner's Ferry. He's in your garage now. I would get rid of him in a day or so or your garage is going to have a ripe odor."

I grinned, "Don't worry. If the county doesn't want him tomorrow I'll ask you to drop him about a hundred miles offshore."

He said, "Your instincts are good. The mix seems unusually potent. Stolen racehorse, black wizard, white supremacists, dead body. This is the best lead I have on the wizard I'm looking for. I'll keep the meeting for you tomorrow. This feels like they have set a trap for you. Say, In your email lure, did you happen to use your real name? Did you send it from your computer?"

Oh damn. I said, "Yes to both."

He said, OK. We have to assume the bad guys know your name and your computer location and they've already set a trap for you. Hold on." He was quiet for a moment. I knew he was in communication with someone far away.

Two people appeared in the kitchen. One big guy dressed in black who reminded me of Gus, and a woman dressed casually, appeared in the kitchen. Lucifer snarled. Bret said, "This is Mack and Samantha, Sam. I have to leave and they will stay with you in case whoever 's interested in you pays a visit. They work with me. They are both wizards and trained bodyguards. Listen to them. I have to go to work now. Get dressed and go to work if you want. If it was me I'd give my employees a couple of days off and hide out. Don't mention magic at all. Tell anyone you want to know that you witnessed a gang hit and these are marshals who will hide you at a safe house until the bad guys are caught. OK? These guys can take you anywhere in the world. They'll take Lucifer with you. You should go to my HQ. Bye." He vanished.

I looked at the two and said, "I'm going to get dressed now," and went upstairs. Sam followed me. I still had that bottle of Drambuie and I thought I deserved it.

Chapter 10

I woke up too early to a screeching noise and shaking. Was this it? The 9.0 that was going to shake Seattle into Puget Sound. No. Lynn was yelling something and shaking me. I wrenched myself out from under my covers and pried my eyes open. "What's up," I bleated?"

Lynn said, "There's a huge horse in the backyard and its eating the bushes. Sam was sitting in a chair in the corner, smiling. Some bodyguard. I looked at the clock. 7:45 am. Millie should be at work.

"Lynn, if you'll get me a cup of coffee, I'll try to send the horse home," I said, very soft.

She said, "All right. Hurry."

I called Millie, she answered on the first ring.

"Good morning, Millie. Two things, first, would you call Mr. Carstairs and tell him I recovered Magellan. Ask where he wants it delivered. Yup. He's in my backyard, eating the bushes. Remind him he owes me a bonus. Second, call Dave Sherry at the county prosecutor's office, tell him I found Ralph Henry. He's dead, I didn't kill him, ask if he'd like the body and if so, where does he want it. Thanks. 'bye."

I had just hung up when it rang. I put it back up to my ear. "Suzanne Ryder," I said.

It was Mrs. Willoughby next door. She said a horse was in my backyard and sticking his head over the fence and eating her roses. Mrs. Willoughby is has quite precise notions on how the neighborhood should function. She's persistent, annoying, and usually right. Right or not, she's still a pain in the keister.

"Why, Mrs. Willoughby, I'm shocked. Where did he come from? I don't have a horse."

She was explaining what she saw when my cell phone rang. I answered it and ignored Mrs. Willoughby for a moment. It was Millie. She gave me an address. I wrote it down and handed it to Sam. I said, "Sam, would you send the horse in my backyard to this address, please?

Sam smiled and said, "Done." I thanked Millie and hung up the cell phone. I went back to the land line and heard Mrs. Willoughby saying that horses were not allowed in a residential zone. I agreed and asked her to verify that it is really a horse and not a deer. I waited and after a while she said, "I don't understand how, but the horse is gone, as well as several of my rose bushes."

I said, "If he shows up again, we must try and find his owner. Who would let a big animal like that run around our neighborhood?" I hung up.

Lynn brought me a cup of coffee and I told her the horse was gone, and she must have been mistaken, it was only a big, big, deer. Wink.

"OK," she said. "Got it."

"Lynn, we have a problem, I told her, "There are some bad guys who may be looking for me and they may come here. Could you stay with your parents for a couple of days?"

"What's happening, Suzy?"

"Lynn, you know I have visions. Its how I find people and stuff. Well, I was looking for a guy that skipped his trial. I found him, but he's dead. It was a gang hit and I saw the killer. These two are US Marshals who are going to take me to a safe location until the bad guys are caught. The bad guys may know this location. So go through the house and take anything with your name or anything they can use to find you out of here. The good guys will find the bad ones and take them out of circulation, but it may take a few days. Wait for me to call and make sure its me. Ask me something only I would know, like how I hooked you up with Dave. Go get busy. We won't leave until you've gotten everything. If you need something moved to your parent's house, give it to Mack. Go."

She grimaced at me and hurried off without a word.

I dressed and ate some yogurt and an orange. Sam and Mack had already eaten they said so I asked them to teleport me and them to the office. Why use my car if I had a couple of wizards to help? I had them drop us directly in my office. I went out to see Millie and Gus, startled them too. I locked the front door and put up the closed sign.

"Millie, when we're done put your cell phone number on the front door. Type up a sign that says we've gone fishing and for emergencies call your number. Forward the office phone to your cell too, please. Some bad guys may be looking for me. Gus and I and Mack and Sam here are going on a trip and you're should go work from your sister's home if you can. Clear?"

"OK, boss, she said. Be careful. Oh, and Dave Sherry asked for Mr. Henry's body to go to the coroner."

"Yeah. Mack could you move the coffin from my garage to the coroner's lab? Thanks. Gus, there could be several bad guys. Load up your heavy artillery and some body armor. If you have anything for me I'd like it, too."

Gus looked at Mack and Sam, then me. How much room and weight do I get?"

Mack said, "Size and weight don't matter so long as where we put it can take the load. We can take anything, up to and including an MBT."

I asked, "What's an MBT?"

Gus answered, "Main Battle Tank. For us that'd be an Abrams. About sixty tons. Unfortunately, I don't have one of those. Let's go to my place and get you dressed and pick up my gear."

Sam asked, "What's the address?"

We left Gus' car in the garage and Mack took us to Gus' house. He had a house in Rainier Valley, one of the ethnic neighborhoods undergoing gentrification. He gave me a big, heavy camouflage vest he called an IOTV. Anyway he said it gave the best protection. It weighed 30 pounds, at least. It was like carrying a sack of dog food around. Some of the weight was my Glock 17, of course. Gus had several pistols and an M-16 with what he said was a 40mm grenade launcher attached.

"OK," I said to Sam and Mack, "we're ready, let's go see your HQ."

We were standing at a receptionist's station in the lobby of a building. I could see snow covered mountains in the distance and forest in the foreground. A pleasant appearing young woman greeted us. "Good morning, Ms. Ryder and Mr. Allard," she said, "welcome to the Magician's Guild." Ms. Ryder, you are in room 219 and Mr. Allard, room 220. Just take the elevator over there. Ms. Steuben will come see you in an hour." She eyed our vests and Gus' weapons and said, "Don't worry about security. This is a well protected place."

I said, "Thank you and went to the elevator. Sam and Mack had vanished. Our rooms were like small apartments with separate living, kitchen bedroom and bath. My closet and dresser held my clothes. I guess Sam moved them for me.

I left Suzanne in Samantha and Mack's capable hands and went looking for the black wizard in Idaho. I had found Magellan about 20 miles south of Bonner's Ferry. I teleported into Sandpoint, ID to get a feeling for the people and landscape. I bought a coffee in a coffee shop and asked about the area. The waitress was friendly and didn't know of anything unusual. I went to the Bonner County Sheriff's office and flashed my FBI ID. The sheriff was a tall, big boned man who looked to be in good shape despite the desk job.

"Sheriff, "I said, "thanks for seeing me. I'm Special Agent Thorne. I'm up here looking into a horse theft. It was stolen in Washington and trucked into your county. It was a valuable champion race horse worth something over a half million. It was recovered halfway to Bonner's Ferry. There were some unusual aspects of the transportation. It seems a helicopter was used for the last fifty miles of the trip. I was wondering if there were any recent reports of unusual aerial activity in your county?"

"Welcome to Idaho, Agent Thorne. We haven't had any reports of anything unusual, 'less you want to count the crazies."

"Crazies, Sheriff?"

"Yup, a couple of ranchers north of here have reported aliens. Flying men and spaceships that look like cars and trucks. That sort of thing. They've been coming in for a month now. One or two a week. Last week there were four."

"All from the same person?"

"No, that's why I sent a deputy to talk to them. All the reports have two or three people who saw it. There was even a picture, but you know how easy it is to doctor a photo nowadays. All the sightings were from the same area."

I said, "A picture of what?"

The Sheriff said, "The bottom of a trailer, maybe a horse trailer or a boxy moving trailer."

"Can you give me a copy of the crazy reports?"

"Sure." He called someone and asked for the reports then he took me to where a secretary was copying the reports for me. I thanked him and he went back to his office.

I went outside stepped behind a truck, went invisible , raised my shield, and flew north. I increased my sensitivity to traces of magic or leftover spells. I looked for anything unusual as I sped over the forest and pastures. I found a meadow on a low peak with signs of an explosion and fire. There were some tendrils of a magic spell floating around.

Different wizard see spells differently. To me they usually look like colored floating strings or threads. Sometimes they appear as a loosely woven pattern. The shapes and what they connect tell me what the spell was doing. I didn't get any useful data from these strings, except that they were thick. A sign of a strong wizard.

I flew over the farm with the oldest report. I didn't see anyone. I went a mile down the county road and landed. I materialized a silver crown vic with a police radio and gave it government plates. I drove to the farm house and knocked on the door. A middle aged man answered the door. I told him I was with the FBI and was looking into the circumstances around a crime in the neighborhood. I told him I read the report and asked him to show me where he made the sighting. He was happy to show me. He got his wife and they took me around back to their garden.

He stopped at a low rabbit fence and pointed toward a hill to the east. He said, "I was standing right here and Marge was right over there," he pointed inside the fence. I had brought a water hose over and looked up at a noise. I saw two men flying, halfway to that hill and maybe 500 feet up in the air. Not like Superman flies, but standing up. They were moving fast. I called to Marge and she looked up and saw them. They were already past us when I saw them so I don't think they saw us."

I asked, "That's what you saw ma'am?"

She answered, "Yeah. Just like Al said. They were wearing long coats too. They were flapping in the wind."

"OK," I said, "which way were they going?"

Al said, "Due north, right up the valley."

"One more question, can you estimate how fast they were traveling?"

Al said, "I'd say about a hundred miles an hour."

"and you ma'am?"

Marge said, "I think a little faster, maybe one fifty. They were making a whooshing noise as they flew."

I thanked them and said I'd let them know what I found out.

I got in my car and drove a mile away and reported in, "Bret Thorne. I talked to two witnesses who saw two flying men three weeks ago. Traveling north at low altitude, one hundred plus mph. Location about twenty miles north of Sandpoint Idaho. Near I-95 at Elmira, ID. I've got police reports of more sightings in the area. I'll send them to HQ Ops now. Send a canvass team and see if they can map their vector and where it ends. Out."

I went to the place where I had found Ralph Henry's coffin . I hole in the National Forest. away from any road. Had to be a wizard, no one else would haul a coffin and body that far from a road. The site was clean, even to my second sight.

Next I checked out the ranch where I had found Magellan. Nice place with fifteen horses in a pasture. I found a man unloading hay in a barn. He was clean and said the owner, a Denny Petlock had gone to town this morning. He didn't know when he'd be back. He didn't ask to see my ID so I just left.

I dematerialized the car, raised my shield, and turned invisible. I flew north at a thousand feet, memorizing the lay of the land and looking for a wizard's lair. I ran a search grid around Bonner's Ferry and Moyle Springs but saw nothing of note. There must have been a thousand barns of all descriptions in my grid. I estimated if I had five good wizards to help, we could search every building in the area in two days. I'd rather narrow the search a little before I started that. I still had the meeting at Wendle Ford tomorrow. I'd do that before starting an area search.

I reported my plan to HQ and dropped in on Bonner's Ferry to see if the natives had anything useful to say. I stopped in the Boundary Community Hospital and talked to a couple of nurses. No strange cases. I tried Mugsy's Tavern next. The bartender said he'd heard there had been several explosions up in the woods near Meadow Creek a week ago. I visited the Kootenai River Brewing Co. The hunters there said the hunting had gone from great a month ago to terrible last week north of town. One guy said he couldn't even find tracks. He thought the game had all left. Meadow Creek was north and east of town.

There was still lots of daylight left so I flew north and east of town and flew search grid. I found where a large group of men had camped in a spot near Meadow Creek, but it had been abandoned days earlier. There were a few magic tendrils laying around, ugly like long, fat glow worms. I sent the location in to HQ and asked for a search of the area at first light tomorrow. I teleported back to HQ and looked for Suzy.

Chapter 11

Gus came to my room in 45 minutes and Ms. Gloria Steuben knocked on my door right on time. She was carrying a small backpack and handed it to me. She said, "I was told you had a familiar with you. This is for him. Most of the witches here have cats and use these to make sure they don't get separated."

I said, "Thanks, but Lucifer doesn't need this."

Gloria smiled and said, "Its hard for even a familiar to keep up when you've learned to fly and teleport. Just keep it handy."

Fly? Teleport? Me? Shoot. What have I gotten myself into?

We sat around my dining table and talked.

Ms. Steuben started with, "Ms. Ryder, you were referred to us by Mr. Thorne. He reported you had good psionic ability and were untrained. Was he correct?"

I said, cautiously, "I have an ability to find things by getting a vision of it, but that's all."

Ms. Steuben said, "Look, my name is Gloria, can I call you Suzy? This stuff is easier if we're informal."

I said, "Sure, Gloria. Suits me and Gus."

Gloria said, "Great. Almost everyone who comes here only has one thing they can do. They discovered it by accident and enjoyed it so much they never pushed beyond it. I discovered I could read minds when I was ten and was afraid to tell anyone for years. I was discovered after an embarrassing adventure on an airplane. I got trained and now I have a full set of abilities."

"Gloria," I said, I've got a business and a couple of people who depend on me. I couldn't just up and leave them and my friends."

"Being a member of the guild is not a regular job for most people. Its more like being an alumnus of a school. We take classes, we learn how to control our talents and we report magic events we see. You don't need to make any decisions now. Bret said you wanted to talk to a specialist in enchanted objects. Esmerelda is busy until lunch so we'll see her then if that's OK with you. In the meantime, I want you and Gus to meet one of our novice trainers."

Gus said, "I don't need to see anyone. I'm here to guard Suzy. I don't have her talents, anyway."

Gloria said, "Gus, you're wrong. You have psionic ability just like Suzy, You just don't know it. You were a soldier, right?"

Gus admitted, "Yeah."

She persisted, "Do you get a feeling when you're being watched or are in danger?"

He said, "All of us who make it to my age pay attention to our feelings."

She said, "Too right. Those feelings are an indication of a latent talent. Only about one in a thousand people have this talent. Many wizards are soldiers that survived because they can see beyond their senses. One of my talents is to detect witches and wizards. I can see their aura. I can see Suzy's glowing around her just like I can see yours. Your aura is intense. Stronger than most I see. You will be a powerful wizard if you take the training. But, its your choice and as I said, there's no need to decide anything now. Let's go see Jason and he'll show you both how to play with your talents. In an hour you'll be able to do things most people only see in movies."

She stood up and walked to the door. Like zombies, Gus and I followed her into wonderland. She took us to a basement room that looked like a gym for acrobatics. I didn't see anyone at first then a man descended from above and touched down in front of us. He came down in a controlled descent. I looked for the rope, but there wasn't one. He said, "Hi. I'm Jason and you're Suzy and Gus, right?" He had a friendly, open face like a great con man.

"Hi, Jason, Yes, I'm Suzy. You're going to teach us magic?"

"No, no, no. I'm going to show you how to do a few simple things all by yourselves. I'm only here to help you find your own ability."

"Watch."

He slowly rose a foot above the floor. and said, "You both will be doing this in a few minutes. Suzy, you first. Just look at the green wall behind me and don't think of anything else. I'm going to talk to your mind and tell it how to do this.

I looked at the wall and said my mantra to myself, 'om mani padme om,' over and over. I felt a tickle, the faintest of thoughts, like I almost remembered something from long ago.

I heard him say, "Suzy, picture yourself floating six inches above the floor. Get a mental image. Now look at your feet."

I was floating, floating!

Jason said, "Suzy now picture yourself floating toward the back wall, slowly. When you are close, picture yourself turning around and coming back to where you are now. Go."

Damn, it worked. I was flying. When I got back, Jason said, "Now go play. stay low. Dropouts are common when you're first doing something you thought impossible." I went.

Jason said, "Gus, your turn. You've never believed in magic before so its going to be harder to get you started. Close your eyes. Now think of yourself standing on the bank of a stream you want to cross. There's a wooden log over the stream about a foot thick. Lift your right foot and place it on the log. OK, now put your left foot on the log beside the right one. OK open your eyes and look at your feet."

"Shit," said Gus, "this would sure have made my life easier ten years ago."

Jason said, now picture yourself floating toward the far wall. When you get close, turn around and come back. Don't go higher yet.

In twenty minutes, Gus, Jason and I were cavorting in the air all over the gym. We stayed low just in case. This was incredible.

Jason got a stack of traffic cones from a closet and put them on the floor in a big circle. He had us fly no higher than the cones weaving in and out around the course. The first time around I knocked over half the cones. Gus was worse, whew. After an hour both Gus and I made it around the course without knocking over the cones.

I thought we were done, but no. Jason got out some stands and bars like used in dog agility courses and put them in the course with the cones. Now we had to go around the cones and under and over the bars. Another hour and we could navigate this 3D agility course without hitting anything.

Jason said, "Come over here, please." Gus and I joined him on the floor. He continued, "now you have the rudiments of free flight. You'll get better and better as you practice. There are dangers to flight. Some hostile or scared person may shoot at you. So you need to learn how to protect yourselves and not be seen. Your minds can do both those things for you, raise a protective shield around you and make you invisible. When you get good at the shield you can forget body armor. The shield is much more effective. OK I'm going to teach your minds both things now, so try to empty them so I can work."

Again that tiny tickle in my thoughts.

Jason picked up two sponge balls from the floor. "Now get a picture of a stone wall around you about two feet away and these balls bouncing off it." He threw a ball at me and it bounced from my invisible wall. I was elated and danced a little jig.

Jason threw the other ball at Gus and it flew across the room like it was shot from a cannon.

I gasped at the force. Jason said, "That's why I use a nerf ball. I used a basketball my first time with a soldier and he broke my arm. I had to go see a healer. Soldiers react with a lot of force to anything that might be dangerous. This stuff you're learning is very powerful. Learning how to keep it under control is the hardest part."

Gus was smiling and said, "Jason, you're right, this stuff is fun.

Jason said, I'm going to show you how to become invisible. Empty your minds again so I can tell you how to do the invisible think. I emptied my mind and got that tiny tickle deep inside.

"Now," Jason said, "same drill as before. make an image of yourself standing in the gym and remove yourself from the image. Good. Open your eyes and look at your hand. Don't move. Its tricky to learn how to walk when you can't see yourself. Its a lot easier if you levitate a few feet."

I couldn't see myself or Gus and I tried to take a step. I almost fell over. I raised myself off the floor and Gus bumped into my back.

"Oops, sorry. I didn't see you," said Gus.

Jason said, "That's all I'm going to show you today. Land and turn visible. OK, good to meet you two. You're excellent students. I'll probably see you later. Goodbye." He left and Gloria came in.

She said, "Well Gus, Suzy. That's real magic. How do you feel?"

Gus said, "Like I felt after my first parachute jump. Ecstatic but worried they might make me do it again."

I said, "Its like the first time I visited Disney world. I'm exhausted, but I want to see everything else."

Gloria said, "It can be draining. Let's go get lunch and meet Esmerelda."

I agreed wholeheartedly and we followed her up to the first floor cafeteria.

I got a salad and roll and soft drink. Gus got a double burger with fries, a piece of blueberry sour cream pie and coffee. Gloria led us to a table with a woman already seated. She introduced us to Esmerelda. Gus sat across from her and I sat beside her.

Esmerelda reminded me of Morticia Addams. Tall, long dark hair, nice breasts and dressed in a black dress. She seemed nice. Gus and I waxed eloquent over our lessons with Jason. Gus was almost stuttering with his urgency. I can only imagine what a shock it must have been for a solid, down to earth soldier to discover magic. To learn he had superpowers. He could fly. and still half believed he was dreaming.

I had known I got visions since high school and I was kind of used to the concept, the existence of an extra ability. It was still sinking in that I could do more. Gus was like a 'been there, done that, got the t-shirt' kid that discovered there was a Santa Claus.

After we had wound down, Esmerelda said, "I understand from Bret that you have an enchanted ring. You want clarification on its properties and consequences. Can I see it?"

I said, "Here it is." and held my hand out to her.

"What do you know about it," she asked?

"I found it in a desk drawer in an envelope . The word 'Asmodeus' was written on the envelope in my mother's hand. She passed on several years ago and she was a witch. In the envelope was the ring and a slip of paper. It said, **"When your eyes watch your object, to your rhyme they will be subject."** I put the ring on and several times I used it to enhance romantic attraction between two people and it works. I discovered after the first night that it had shrunk and I couldn't remove it."

She held my hand and studied the ring closely. She said, "I can see the aura from it and it has indeed shrunk to fit your finger too snug for removal. I recommend you not try to cut it. These enchanted objects sometimes have protective spells woven in. Asmodeus is a demon of first rank. If he enchanted the ring or is inhabiting it any attempt at removal would be hazardous. As the demon of lust he probably wouldn't harm you, but the consequences could be disruptive to you. Its probably best just to not use it. These enchantments usually fade over time."

"How much time," I asked?

"Sorry. No way to tell. Its small, but size is not an important factor with enchantments," Esmerelda said.

This was as far as I had gotten too. So I said, "Thanks. I'll treat it like a regular ring and see if it dies away. Bret and you know each other?"

She smirked, "Oh, yes we go way back."

"Tell me about him. I've only spoken to him twice and he's kind of overpowering."

"Yeah," she said "I found the best way to deal with him is to tickle him in the ribs. He falls apart and is easier to be around afterwards."

I smiled and said, "Tickling sounds like a peaceful solution. Thanks." But I was not smiling inside. Had they been lovers? Were they still lovers? Was he the kind of guy with a girl in every port? Oh shit. How can I ask that?

I said, "Mr. Thorne seems to think I'm in danger from some bad wizards. That's why I'm here. Does he get overreact sometimes. I guess what I'm asking is, how likely is it he's right?"

Gloria looked at Esmerelda and said, "Esme, you know him much better than I. What do you think?"

Esmerelda said, "He's exasperating, close lipped, the strong, silent type. But he's usually right on. I trust him."

Here's the question. I asked, "I just met him. How well do you know him?"

She said, I've known him all my life. I know him as well as you can know a man."

Chapter 11

Oh no. Childhood sweethearts. I can't ask her anything else or I'll give him away. I'll break our affair off as soon as I see him. Its the ring. I never sleep with a man I've just met. It must have been Asmodeus' enchantment.

We finished lunch and Gloria took us back to the gym to practice and left us. I looked at the big room and tried to remember everything I had done an hour ago. I was so afraid of messing up and crashing. I said, "Gus, lets try out our stuff on the ground first," and picked up the nerf ball.

Gus said, "OK Suzy. My shield's up. Make sure yours is before you toss the ball."

"Roger, its up." I tossed the ball at Gus. It bounced three feet in front of him. in thin air. It flew back toward me like a rocket and bounced off my shield. I realized shield were one way. I could throw something through mine and it deflected things coming at me. I watched the nerf ball bounce back and forth between our shields like a video game.

Gus said, "Hey. Our shields reflect, they don't deflect. And they increase to velocity of whatever they reflect. This means if someone shoots at us with a gun, the bullet's going to be reflected back at the shooter, even faster. They will be shot with their own gun. I wonder if we can control which way the shield sends things?"

"Who cares. If someone shoots at me, its only fair that they get shot."

"Suzy, sometimes you don't want the guy who shoots at you to be dead. Sometimes you want to talk to them."

"OK, Gus. Good point. Let's try invisibility now. Don't move." He vanished. "Can you see me?"

I heard his voice, "Yep. Gone. Me too?"

I answered, Yes, you're gone. Turn it off before you fly." I turned mine off. When he reappeared, I took off and he followed. We played follow the leader and tag and flew in formation. We got the nerf ball and played catch from all the weird angles we could think of. We were still pretty sloppy fliers. But Jason said we were doing fine, just like all his students and we needed practice.

I found Suzy and Gus in the gym. I was pleased to see they both were zipping around like drunken sparrows in the big space. I stood inside the door and watched for a moment then Suzy spotted me and dove at me like a falcon after lunch. She slowed perfectly, I grabbed her when she was ten feet out and cushioned her landing. She landed lightly in my arms, and wrapped herself around me. We kissed and she tasted like heaven. No, I decided, not heaven, she tasted like home. I liked her a lot. I avoided the "L..." word because it had caused folks I knew a world of hurt. I hoped if I ever "L...ed" someone, it would feel like this. I'd slept with a few girls and felt lusted for a few more, but this felt special and lasting.

When we broke the kiss I said, "Hi, Suzy. Miss me or were you having too much fun?"

She was breathless and gasped, "Bret, I've missed you terribly. But this is out of this world. I can fly. I'm getting good at it. I landed perfectly in your arms. I can mostly go where I aim. Jason says we need practice to improve. Would you fly with me? Now? Outside? Can we take Gus. He's real good too."

It seemed like a good idea so I said, "OK. I'm going to take you and Gus to a safe place to practice." I teleported us to Protection Island. Its a federal wildlife preserve in the Straits of Juan de Fuca, just off the Washington coast. The only inhabitant is a caretaker biologist that I know. He's one of our reserve wizards and I drop in whenever I'm in the area. I told them, "this island is a wildlife sanctuary. The resident biologist is a friend of mine. Play around over or near the island. Airplanes are supposed to stay above 2000 feet over the island. I'm going to go see my friend. I'll be back soon. You should stay together. Practice your invisibility if you want to get close to the wildlife or if you see any people, like in a boat. Have fun." I teleported to see Henry.

I dropped in outside his cottage and knocked. He was glad for the company and we sat outside and knocked back a couple or brews. He filled me in on his station. He was our watcher over the straits of Juan de Fuca. A wide channel from the Pacific into Puget Sound. There was a lot of ship traffic here. He would report a large shipment of illegal drugs but left the small ones alone. Not his idea or mine. Policy from HQ.

While we were sipping, I received a report from Idaho. About thirty white supremacists have disappeared in the last two weeks. Not whole groups, just a couple from each known group. Two of the vanished men were suspected of having latent talents. Hints of latent talents are one of the key things our watchers look for. We want to identify as many of these as we can. Even if they're harmlessly using their talent to dowse for water. Some develop into threats in the future with the right stimulus.

"Gus, I said, "let's play tourist and fly around the island and see what we can find."

He replied, "OK, boss, lead on."

Protection Island is an irregular blob of land maybe a mile long and a half mile wide. Most of it is a plateau with steep cliffs on the north side filled with seabird nests. The eastern tip is a long, low spit. I turned invisible and flew slowly along its length. It was covered in sea lions sunning themselves. Then we flew over the cliffs and startled a few birds with our wake.

I found them flying over the northern cliffs looking at the bird nests. I settled in a little above and behind them and said, "Nice day for a flight, guys."

They twitched and stopped. They still had their shields up and were cloaked. I was in the same state. Suzy said, "Where are you and how can you see us?"

"Hi. You have just scratched the surface in your education. Its like driving a car. You've learned to make it go where you want and stop. And you're good at it. But you've only learned tried four controls. There's still all the other switches to learn. Right now you're invisible to people without a talent. Any witch or wizard can see you right now. You need a little more training to learn how to turn off the lights on your car. I can tell your shields are in good shape, you're invisible to most people and you're flying well. Let's fly to your house, Suzy. Follow me."

I went up to three thousand feet and took a course of 135 degrees magnetic. A beeline course. It was about thirty five miles to Suzy's house and I kept my speed down to two hundred mph. I started descending at the West Point sewage treatment plant. It took about ten minutes and I pointed out some of the sights. I enjoyed playing tour guide. They both knew the area but had never even been in a light plane. I brought us to a soft landing on her front porch.

Gus was ready to go home so I teleported him back to the office. He was going to get his car and drive it home. I bet he didn't use it too much from now on.

Suzy and I went inside and she released Lucifer. He was happy to be home too and went off to see if the mouse farm he'd been raising had any new babies for him. We sat on the couch in her living room and looked at the city lights. She cuddled into my arm and I materialized two glasses of Drambuie.

Suzy said, "I never knew how convenient a wizard could be. I'll have to have you over more often."

I said, "Its nice to relax with a beautiful woman and a glass of liqueur after a long day. Makes me appreciate life. You had a busy day too. Tell me about it."

Suzy said, "Oh, you know. Pretty mundane. Gus and I went to a class and picked up a few new skills. I don't think there's much of a market for these skills. I just haven't seen any ads for people that fly. Maybe I can be a stunt woman in a movie. Save the cost of all those wires and cranes. Or a profession. We'd be impressive thieves."

"Good idea. There's probably a career opportunity in smuggling, too. Land anywhere you want, invisible, bulletproof. That could work. Of course you'd have pretty unsavory characters for clients. You'd have to keep your shield up all the time."

Suzy finished her glass and I set it on the table. She stood up and said, "I have something to show you. Come up to my room in five minutes, please."

She went upstairs and I followed in five minutes. Before I went up I put a screen around the house to wake me for intruders or spells. I would put up a shield around the bed before I went to sleep.

I had a tiny black thong on with a transparent panel and a transparent black chemise. Together they hid exactly nothing. I looked at myself in the mirror. I looked like an expensive hooker. Lucifer looked at me and purred approvingly.

I put on a robe and waited. Then I heard Bret climb the stairs. He knocked on the door. I opened it and said in a soft voice, "Bret, I just had to show you some things you've not seen before. Come in. I want to see if you like them."

He smiled and said, "I'm quite sure I will like them. Let's see."

I parted my lips and let a little tongue show, like I was worried he wouldn't like it. Then I opened my robe and let it drop to the floor. I lifted a knee and cocked my hips. I rotated my torso away from the lifted knee, just a little. I put my hands behind my head and asked, "is this too risqué?"

"Oh, no, Suzy. Its perfect. Say, you wouldn't be trying to seduce me, would you?"

"No, sir," I said in my best little girl voice. " I'm sure A nice girl wouldn't do that. That's naughty."

"So true, Suzy. I think you might be a little naughty, don't you?"

"Maybe just a little, sir. Do you think I should be spanked?"

"That would be fitting. Please remove those scandalous clothes, Julie."

They were on the floor in a flash and he took my hand and led me to the bed. He sat on the edge and pulled me down across his lap. He put a leg over mine and rubbed my ass. I never felt anything so good in my life. My pussy revved up and started making me wet.

He said, "You know, Suzy, I haven't done this before, so I may not get it perfect this time. I may need more practice later."

I purred, "I'm sure I will need some correction in the future."

"Good." His hard hand swatted my left ass cheek. It stung but not nearly so much as I wanted.

I said, "Sir, that was a good start, but I need to feel it even more to change my ways. A little harder would be most beneficial to me."

"I was just testing my swing. Now I think it will be best if you thank me and count the spanks. Let's try it. His hand landed, at least twice as hard, on my right ass cheek. My ass burned and I felt my love juices flow into my pussy.

I squealed and said, "Two. Thank you, sir. I think you've got it."

I started moaning in pleasure on number five. I couldn't stop myself. I just felt so horny.

On number six, I said, "Six, Thank you, sir. I want you Bret. I'm ready."

He ignored me. My moans got louder and My need grew with every swat of his hand. I felt like I would explode.

After twenty he stood up and lay me face up on his bed. I spread my legs and raised my arms to pull him down on me. He said, "put your hands behind your head and keep them there. My pussy spasmed at his control. I felt the joy of submission to him as I put my hands in place.

He undressed and shoved a pillow under my ass. His rampant cock nudged at my nether lips. I spread my legs as far apart as I could. spreading my labia lips open. He took my ankles in his strong hands and lifted my legs over my head until I was as open as possible. I felt his cock slip into me. The slippery friction on my love canal was breathtaking. I moaned and felt him bottom out. Then he began his in and out cycle. Each stroke took me closer to my orgasm until he flung me over the edge. My belly clenched around his cock, increasing the friction and my pleasure as he kept pumping me up. I went even higher and my second orgasm was fantastic. It far overshadowed my first. I was close to fainting it was so powerful. He kept pumping and I was pushed to my limit. He climaxed in a great flood of hot spend inside me. Then I orgasmed yet again in a mighty flood of juice and such joy. The pleasure was so intense I fainted. I awoke alone on the bed and saw him standing over me. Magnificently naked, a man such as maiden dreams only imagine.

He said, "You are every bit as good in bed as you looked today. And you looked better than every woman in Seattle."

I replied, dreamily, "Thank you sir. Does this mean I may get a return engagement sometime in the future?"

He smiled and said, "Return? You surely don't think you are done tonight, do you. I think you are in need of extra correction. Perhaps for the foreseeable future."

He lay down beside me and rolled me over on top of him. Already he was ready to go again. Robust is a good word to use. He set me onto his cock and my pussy responded in an instant. I could feel my love juices running down my love canal. He started me going up and down with his hands. My legs got the idea and I bounced and bounced. My first orgasm came fast. He got his first and my second was right behind him.

I slumped off him and we both slept for a while. I woke up again when he straddled me in the wee hours. I was glad to feel him in me again. I didn't have to wait long to enjoy my next one. We each had one orgasm this time. That night I counted seven orgasms with two being superlative.

Suzy had set the meeting for 11 am at a Ford dealer in Spokane. I got Sam and Mack and we went there at ten to survey the site. I made them a Ford van with "Washington Ford Dealers Association" painted on both sides. I put a new F-150 beside it. I cast a visual spell on Samantha so she looked like Suzanne. I went into the dealership and flashed my FBI credentials. I asked them to avoid the van and pickup in their north parking lot. I also advised them to stay inside around 11. We were conducting a sting and planned to arrest a gentleman. They were happy to help. This was Eastern Washington, a very conservative area.

Sam looked in the mirror and said, "Bret, your memory of Suzy is not too accurate. I think you exaggerated her measurements and her hair."

I replied, "You're just jealous, Sam. If you want, I can help you a little. You won't feel a thing."

She said, "You're a dirty old man. If I want to improve myself, I'll do it myself. No guy is going to go poking around my body."

"Yeah, wait until you find a good lover."

At 10:45 Sam and Mack got out of the van. Mack held a large video camera with microphone. I positioned myself on the roof of the dealership. I made sure we all had our shields raised and I went invisible. At 10:57 a black van pulled up close to our van. I scanned it and sensed danger. I alerted Sam and Mack "There's six men in the van. One has a masking spell like yours Sam."

I cast my sense of perception wide around the dealership. I found four more black vans scattered around the periphery. They were disgorging men fast. All of the men wore suits and were armed with handguns.

I alerted Sam and Mack, "Twenty more armed men approaching from all around the lot. If any show a weapon, try to stun them. We need to talk to them."

I stayed invisible and flew out to the edge of the lot. If they fired anything at me, I didn't want innocent bystanders in the line of fire. I looked down at Sam and Mack. They had dropped the first six. One's neck was at a funny angle. The others looked asleep.

The other men were running at Sam and Mack. They were quiet all had their guns out of sight. A flurry of lightning bolts flew from some of the attackers toward Sam and Mack. They bolts bounced harmlessly off their shield. If the attackers got close enough they could swamp Sam and Mack's shields by sheer volume.

I threw up a wall of fire between my folks and the attackers. When the heat stopped them, I started knocking out the ones in back. I had fifteen down before the bright ones flew high enough to see over the flames. Finally someone detected me and flung a bolt at me. My shield handled it easily. I saw the one who found me was a witch. She flew off to the east as soon as she flung her bolt. I told Sam and Mack to stay defensive. I continued knocking them out. Now I had to lower them to the ground so the fall didn't kill them. Finally, the last one was down.

I looked for the one that flew away, but couldn't find her. We put the attackers back in their vans and sent them to HQ for interrogation.

I got a cell call from Gus and answered it, "Thorne."

Gus yelled, "A wizard came to the office and took Suzy. You've got to find her."

A cold chill roared through my body. "Gus, what did he look like?"

Like you. Big guy. All in black. Long black hair. Sinister smile. Long black leather coat. No hat. Caucasian but dark complexion. Six-five, 225 pounds. Moved very fast. He could have been your ugly twin."

I spoke absently, "Bart. Calls himself Sauron."

Part 3 : Sauron

Chapter 12

I was at my desk doing some paperwork when I felt a hand on my shoulder. I thought it was Bret from his silent entry. I said, "I'm glad you came. I have some questions about locations." I looked at his hand and saw a black glove. I was startled since he had never worn gloves before. I turned in my chair and screamed. It wasn't Bret. He was as big, but he was dressed all in black and had long black hair.

He said, "Sorry to disappoint you, my dear."

Gus flung open the door and saw the stranger. He had a gun in his hand. Gus lifted his hand and the gun disappeared. The stranger laughed derisively and everything went black.

I was in a brightly lit workshop. There were a couple of men in work clothes and the stranger standing beside me still holding my shoulder. I had been frightened just a moment before but I felt much better now. I knew the man in black had my best interest at heart. I was happy to be here. A woman I didn't know dressed in a black leather catsuit came in the room and said, "Hello, Suzy. We're so glad you're here. Say aren't you hot? Its so hot in here."

She was right. I was hot. Too hot. I needed to cool down.

She said, "Suzy, you're sweating. Let's get rid of those hot clothes. You're sweltering."

I stood up and she helped me get rid of those too hot clothes. I tossed them on the floor and kicked them away. I said, "Away hot clothes. I want to be cool."

It felt so good to have the cool air flowing over my body. I looked down and giggled. I was naked. I looked good. I felt my breasts and my tummy and I felt good.

She said, " You're a beautiful girl, Suzy. You shouldn't hide your beauty under all those clothes.

I agreed with her. I said, You too. You shouldn't wear all those clothes either. You should take them off too. We can be beautiful together."

She said, "Good idea, but let's get your jewelry done first, OK?"

I was so happy she agreed with me. I said, Okey dokey. Is this a jewelry store?"

She said, Its where they make jewelry and these men are going to make some just for you. They'll make sure no one else can wear your stuff. OK?"

I felt glad it be all mine. I said, And I can keep it? Always?"

She said, "Of course, Suzy. Its just for you and you will always have them. Now walk over to the bench with me."

She took my hand and led me to a workbench. It was a clean workbench with lots of tool on a pegboard and many cabinets.

I stood on a little bench and the smith measured my ankles and waist and neck. Just like a tailor and wrote everything down. He said he was going to make my anklets first. I watched the smith work, turning a plain length of steel into a work of art any girl would be proud to wear. I judged it beautiful. They lifted my right leg and placed my ankle in the opened circlet of steel. A large vise closed it. I felt its snug grip on my ankle. I was glad it fit so well. That was a sure sign of good workmanship.. The smith's hammer sung its song. When he finished, the rivets held the anklet snug on my ankle. He ordered me to stand and checked the fit. The smith judged it good and started on my other anklet.

The other anklet was soon snug. They were beautiful and I bent my legs to examine my new jewelry. I told the woman, "These would make great leg irons. They are so much nicer than the ones slaves had to wear. Could I try that sometime. I bet its hard to run in leg irons."

She said, "Of course you can try it. She asked the smith if he would put a chain between my anklets. He smiled when he said, "I've got just the right chain for that." I sat on the stool and put my feet up on an anvil and with a few whacks of his hammer, a shiny silver chain joined my anklets. It added a lot to my anklets. Now when I walked it glittered and clattered so everyone would look at my new jewelry. I was proud of them. The woman held my arm as I walked around the shop. It was not so hard. I loved the sound of the chain when I took a step. We stopped in front of a mirror so I could look. They were beautiful. I kicked a foot to watch the chain glitter in the light and clatter on the floor.

I said, "Thank you for my anklets. They're beautiful and look so nice on me."

She said "I'm glad you like them. But we're not done. We're going to make you a necklace too."

I was overjoyed. I asked, "Just like my anklets?" I giggled

She said, "Just like." She led me back to the smith. I was so happy I skipped. I hadn't done that since I was ten. It turned out leg irons don't affect skipping.

I watched him make my necklace. It was wider than I expected, more of a torc or collar. Still beautiful though. When he finished decorating it, he held it up so I could see it. It was wide, gleaming silver, curved out of a single piece of steel. There was no hinge. The opening was just wide enough to slide around my neck. It had a thick staple welded to the center with a large, thick steel ring. My name, "Suzanne" was engraved around the staple. Joy soared in me. This was mine. No one else would ever wear it. I could never lose. Only a smith could remove it. I was so lucky.

I stared at my necklace. It was obdurate, beautiful, and heavy and obdurate. I would wear it for the rest of my life. For an instant I wondered what I would do if I wanted to remove it. Silly, why would I ever want to lose something so beautiful? I wanted to wear it. I longed for its cold embrace tight on my throat

They clamped the collar into a large machine and I lay upon its cold surface. My neck was inserted into it and the machine closed the collar. It was like a large, smooth hand claiming me. When closed, I could feel it touching every inch of my neck in a snug grip. They inserted the rivets and hammered them flat. The surface was filed and polished to a perfect flatness.

I lay there for many minutes feeling the vibrations of the work that fastened my necklace upon me. I couldn't move and felt more feminine than I ever had before. I verified that my necklace was heavy. I lifted my head and sat up. The woman helped me to stand and led me back to the mirror. It was beautiful and was perfect on me. It was exactly right for me.

I said, "What's your name?"

She said , " Its Salome."

I said, "Thank you Salome for this wonderful jewelry. I'm so happy."

Salome said, "We have just one more item. Lift your arms please."

She held up a steel belt with a metal plate hanging from two short chains.

I put my hands on top of my head and watched as she wrapped the belt around my waist. She pulled the plate up between my legs and locked it to the front of the belt. A lock snapped and the belt gripped me tight. I couldn't take a full breath the belt was so tight.

Salome said, "Now wriggle the belt around until its comfortable."

I lowered my arms and pushed and pulled, but it barely moved. "Is this jewelry too," I asked?

Salome said, "Of course. Many women wear these to protect their virginity and to look good. See how the gleaming chrome has the same shine as you necklace and anklets? Say, Aren't you getting cold. Would you like something to wear?"

I agreed, "Yes, I'd like something to wear."

Salome said, "Lift your arms and she dropped some cloth over me. My arms went out the openings and I was dressed. Simple and convenient. I didn't need panties with the chastity belt. I looked down and saw I was wearing a burlap sack with holes for my arms and head. Neat. I had never worn one of these before. This was such fun. New clothing, new jewelry and the people were so nice.

Salome said, time for bed now." She took my hand and led me through several doors, down a hallway and into a bedroom. There were lots of beds and most had a woman sleeping on them. She took me to an open bed and said, "Lay down here, Suzy. You can meet your new friends tomorrow. Goodnight."

"Good night, Salome." It was wonderful having such nice friends. I was so happy.

I woke up, coming instantly alert. I had been kidnapped. I remembered Gus and his gun disappearing and the laugh of the wizard. Wait. I remembered being incredibly happy last night. I remembered my silly vacuous comments. He had drugged me. How much of what I remembered was real? I was laying on a cot in a room with a white ceiling. I turned my head and saw Lucifer laying beside me and looking at me. How? "Never mind, Suzy," I told myself. I looked over him and saw there were more cots in the room and several women. I sat up and felt the heavy weight on my neck. I lifted my hands and felt. I was wearing a steel collar with a big ring. I swung my legs off the cot and discovered my feet were shackled. I was wearing a scratchy burlap bag for a dress. There was something hard pressing into my waist . I lifted the hem of the burlap bag and found a chastity belt. Shiny, chrome, and locked. I felt fine, physically, and violated emotionally. I wanted to scream but saw several of the women looking at me. I held my emotions in check and asked, reasonably calmly, "What the hell is going on here?"

On second glance all the women I could see were collared and shackled. I couldn't tell about the chastity belt.

A pretty blonde said, "We've been captured by a bunch of men and women. They don't tell us anything. We all woke up here like you, and we all have chastity belts locked on us like you. I saw you peek at it. I'm Molly. I've been here two weeks. The others mostly shorter."

"Where are we?"

Molly answered, "We don't know. We were all taken at home or work, or school and they knocked us out somehow. We woke up here just like you see us."

"Do they ever let you out of the room?" I asked.

A different girl with brown hair said, "They take us out every day to work. We do the cooking for the men."

"Do you get to go outside?"

Molly answered, "Never. They just take us to the kitchen and dining room and we make meals and serve the men. We have to clean our quarters."

"How many men?

Brown haired girl said, " The most I've seen is thirty. There are tables and chairs for a lot more. There's a woman with the men. Wears a leather cat suit. She seems to be in charge when the boss is gone. There's a bunch of other women we see sometimes. They're fixed just like us, except no chastity belts. Some of them are foreigners and don't speak much English. I think the men have sex with them."

"Who's the boss?"

"Big, scary dude," said Molly, "he always wears black and never, ever, smiles. Everyone except the woman is scared of him."

"Yeah," I said, "I met him. What are the other men like? Wait, don't answer that. First, tell me your names and where you live, please."

The brown haired girl said, "I'm Pat." The other girls said their names and I tried to memorize them. There were nine of us all together. Me, Molly, Pat, Sue, Sharon, Alicia, Ginger, Corinne, and Julie. Most of them came from Idaho. Alicia and I came from Washington.

"OK," I said, "talk about the men."

Sue spoke up, "they seem like regular guys. They talk big, like always, but they're nice to us. They don't talk rough that I've heard. and they never touch us. But I think they'd like to from the looks they give us. They're all afraid of the boss."

I saw the girls nodding their heads in agreement.

Ginger said, "I think a bunch of them are white supremacists. When I was cleaning near a group I heard them talking about getting all the colored folks out of the country. It was talk like I always hear around home."

I asked, "What do they do here?"

Molly said, "They're here for training. I heard them and I saw the woman teaching them something in the dining hall. She was talking about how to feel things with their mind. It didn't make a lot of sense, but they were all paying attention. If they had paid as much attention in school, they'd all be lawyers or scientists now."

I wondered out loud, "So I wonder why we are in chastity belts and the other women aren't. Don't we get to have some of the good times too?"

Sue said, I was with there other girls and they gave us some sort of weird test and then I got put in the belt and in here."

"What kind of test?" I asked.

Sue thought a moment and then asked, "Did you ever see the movie 'Ghostbusters?'"

"Yes."

"Well, it was like the test Dr. Vinkman gave the pretty girl at the start of the movie. Guessing cards you can't see, plus some other stuff like that."

So only women with talents were in this room. The guy who kidnapped me matched their description of the boss. He was clearly a wizard. I had a sinking feeling we were all members of the boss' harem. He was going to use us to make witches and wizards for him. Unless he already had. My feelings sunk even lower.

Molly said, Its almost time for us to get lunch ready. They'll come for us. Just do what they say or you'll get whipped. Its no big deal."

Moments later the only door in the room opened and Salome and two men entered. Salome had a whip coiled on her belt. It was a perfect accessory for her cat suit. She said, "Lunch time girls. Line up. Single file."

I considered fighting back. After all I had a shield and could turn invisible and could fly. I decided to wait. What I had was stealth. I hadn't learned anything I could use to attack with. I didn't know what was outside this room either. I needed knowledge before I acted. I would only get one chance. She stood by the door and the men walked down the line locking a long chain to our collars. When they were done there was a length of chain hanging at both ends of our line. One man took each end of the chain and led us out the door. We all had heavy chains joining our ankles and were noisy. The clattering and clinking was loud and demeaning.

Chapter 13

This was my first experience with the coffle. It was much more demeaning than it sounds like. I had read stories where it was described, but its impact on me was breathtaking. Even with my hands free I was more confined than in the room. I could only move in unison with the rest of the coffle. I couldn't kneel or stand or walk unless we all moved together. There were nine young, healthy women on the coffle. We were easily controlled by two guards. Heck, one was enough. All our education and fitness and desire were useless against the collar and chain. We learned to coordinate our motions to move smoothly with our neighbors. Failure meant jerks of all our necks and whips striping our asses for clumsiness. I hated it, but couldn't help but see it as a definition of femininity in a man's world. A world where might made right. If Bret had put it on me I would have not hated it. I knew some submissive women enjoyed wearing the collar of their men. From Bret it wouldn't have been unwelcome, at least in private. I thought about him locking me in his collar and felt arousal. No. I rejected the thought. I was not his property. I was his girlfriend, his lover. I wanted to be more than that, but not his slave. His partner. Yes.

It was a short walk down a concrete walled hall. Then we were in the dining hall. We walked on into the kitchen. It was simple fare. We made tuna salad sandwiches, salad, green beans. Cake and ice cream for desert. The men came in and lined up cafeteria style and we ladled food onto their plates. It was hard to be angry at them. They were polite and thanked us for the food. I suspected they were only a little happier to be here than I was.

The incongruity of the situation was hard to grasp. Nine women chained together by the neck, shackled, dishing food out to a cafeteria line of men. Why the hell wasn't I mad? Lasting effects of the drug yesterday?

Lucifer sat on top of a refrigerator and watched us. No one else seemed to see him. He must have some power of selective invisibility?

When we were finished serving the men, Salome told us to get our own food. The two men had eaten with the others and were sitting at a table. She had us get what we wanted then led us out to a table. We sat around it, linked to our neighbors by the long chain. There was four or more feet between each girl. The woman said we would get to use the restroom when we got back to our room. She ate with us.

I steeled myself and asked her, "You're in charge here but I don't know what to call you. Can you tell me?"

She said, "My name is Salome. You can use that or Ms. or Ma'am, so long as you are respectful."

"I was drugged yesterday when you put all this hardware on me. Can you tell me what it was?"

"Nope, she said, "it wasn't a drug. It was a spell Sauron put on you when he brought you here. It makes you more compliant and very happy."

Now some real questions, "Ma'am, can you tell us how long we will be here?"

She said, "There is not a precise answer for that. We will be here until Sauron's project is over. That could be a week or a month. Probably no longer. After that we'll go elsewhere."

"Ma'am, I asked, "will he let us go when he's done here?"

She looked sad and said, "I'm afraid not. You are all part of a longer term project. You will probably never be released. He will always take good care of you, though, but you've been chosen for a project."

There were gasps and exclamations all around the table. Several girls wailed, "I don't want to stay here." "I've got a husband and child at home." Even, "I'm almost done with my degree."

When they had run down, I asked, "Aren't you his wife?"

She looked even sadder and said, "No, I'm not. And I'm not in his project, either. I'm his assistant."

I could see she was unhappy with the arrangement. I said, "So you can leave whenever you want?"

She said, "Yes, I guess I could, but I'm hoping he will come to care for me more than my ability. If I could, I'd send you all home and take your place. But his ideas are rather firmly set."

I asked, "Are these chastity belts part of his plan for us?"

Salome said, "Yes. Isn't it obvious? You're reserved for him. He wants you to make babies with talent. You all have at least a latent talent. With the proper seed you will all be his little factory to make wizards and witches. The belts are to ensure no other man gets their seed in you while he's away."

Molly said, "But..but...That's terrible. Its barbaric."

Salome said, "He intends to take good care of you. Pampered breeders, that's you. The practice is steeped in tradition. Western Kings and royalty used to lock their women in belts like yours. To ensure no one made a bastard child in his wife while he was out of town. Yours are much more comfortable than the early ones.

We cleaned the kitchen and got ready for dinner. They marched us back to our room and the chain removed. Salome brought us some old magazines and some books to read. I spent half of the time before dinner in the bathroom trying to learn how to clean my chastity belt.

The chastity belt was not comfortable. The waist band was very tight and dug into my skin. It was impossible to take a deep breath. The metal plate wasn't an exact fit for my bones. It pinched my skin over my pelvic bones if I stepped wrong. I complained but was told not to step that way. Duh. The slit for my pee worked OK, but I always got a little inside that toilet paper couldn't reach. They gave us sanitary wipes that were thin enough to reach inside a little ways. I learned to sit very erect when I crapped. If I slouched even a little, I'd soil the point of the metal plate where the two chains attached. Just going to the bathroom took forever to get clean. No matter how thoroughly I cleaned, a little aroma became apparent after two or three days of wearing it. The showers had wands so I could flush it out good. Taking a shower every time I used the toilet meant most of my day was in the bathroom.

Every couple of days Salome would take it off and clean us thoroughly. On cleaning day Salome and two men would come in our room and cuff one wrist to our beds. Then the two guards would leave and she'd take us in the bathroom, one at a time. We would take off our sack dresses then she'd cuff our hands together. She'd pull them over our head, and lock them to our collar. Then she'd unlock the chastity belt and remove it. We'd climb in the shower and she'd wash us thoroughly. It felt good to be clean again. Someone else washing my privates made me aroused and embarrassed by my traitorous body. Then she'd wash the belt, dry us off, dry the belt off and put it back on us. She'd unlock our hands, take us back in the room, and cuff us to our bed. When we were all clean, the guards would come back and unlock us.

We had a large bathroom with cosmetics. We tried to look as good as we could for our own morale. I tried getting a vision of Bret or any of the people I met at MG HQ. There must have been a magic shield around the whole place cause I could never see anything.

Lucifer would come and go as he pleased. I guess he was exploring and finding food. The other girls would pet him and try to play with him, but he remained regal, aloof. They never commented when he wasn't there. Maybe they didn't notice? Bret said he understood English. I wonder if he'd help with my escape plans. "Won't hurt to try," I thought."

The next time he was on my cot, I said, "Lucifer, I need some cloth to wrap around the girl's ankle chains to quiet them. Would you try and get me some. Nine pieces of cloth six inches wide and two feet long."

He looked at me and said, "Ack."

I said, "Thank you, Lucifer."

He jumped down and walked under my cot. I watched for a half hour and he returned with a rolled up piece of cloth in his mouth. He jumped up on the cot and dropped the cloth in my lap. He understood me. He also walks through walls, I guess. I could see a whole new fleet of possibilities opening up for us.

We were all pretty bored. It was a relief to prepare the meals. Most of the time we just sat or lay on the cots. There was nothing else to do. Any attempts at conversation always flipped into worry over our former loves and lives. This must be what its like in prison. Better, I guess because this prison's population is so small. I wondered how large a harem was. I had seen the movie 'Harem' and it was smaller than this. On the other hand, I heard some ancient kings in Persia had harems with one woman for every day of the year.

I was bored and worried. Would Bret be able to find me? What about my business? What is happening with Gus, Lynn, and Millie?

Chapter 14

I mobilized all the resources of MG and set them looking for Sauron and Suzy. I had good records of both their magic and physical personae. The best clues I had were all in Northern Idaho. I went back up there with a forensics team. We scoured the locations where Ralph Henry's body was found. Also the ranch where Magellan was found, and many activity sites around Bonner's Lake.

One thing that nagged me was why was Magellan stolen. What was his connection. I decided it had to be important. I went back to the ranch intending to get some answers out of the owner. The same hired hand told me again that Mr. Petlock was not at home. I decided to see for myself. I left and raised my shield and my cloak then I flew over the house. I hovered and extended my sense of perception. I found a woman in the kitchen and two men in the basement. I teleported into the basement, still invisible and looked at the men. One was in his sixties, thin hair, potbelly. The other was on his thirties, and holding a gun generally aimed toward Mr. Petlock. I took his gun and put him to sleep. Then I materialized in front of Mr. Petlock.

"Mr. Petlock?" I asked.

"Yes," he said, "who are you?"

"FBI," I said, "what's going on here?

"They've been holding my wife and I prisoner in our own house," he said.

"Who is 'They?'"

"Some guy rented a piece of my land. Paid a good price in cash and a horse I wanted, then weird things started happening, so I asked them to move on. They didn't take kindly to that request and put armed guards on us to keep us quiet. Said they'd be gone by the end of the month."

"Mr. Petlock," I asked, "was the horse named Magellan?"

He said, "He's a great horse. That was most of my price for letting the guys use my land. He was delivered a couple of days ago. Have you seen him?"

"Sorry, he was stolen and he's been returned to his owner already."

"You're sure? I didn't hear any trucks."

"I'm sure. He's back in Washington. How much land did they rent with Magellan?"

"A big piece, nearly 50,000 acres east of here up in the mountains."

"Did they say what they wanted it for?"

"They just said it was an exercise for a private security company."

I asked, "How many people do you have working for you? I met your hired hand. He told me you were in town."

"That's not my hired hand. I've only got two men who come in the summer. He's one of them."

"OK, go tell your wife you're OK. I've got a couple of men coming in who'll take car of any more of them who come here. Do you have a place you can go until this is cleared up?"

"Yeah, My son lives in Washington. We can go there."

"Leave your phone number and address with one of my men before you go, please."

He went upstairs and I took the slumbering man to the barn. I put the hired hand to sleep, cuffed them both to a tractor and wrapped a truthfulness spell around them. Then I woke them up. "Hi, guys. I'm Bret Thorne, FBI. You're in a lot of trouble. False imprisonment and kidnapping to start. Who's your leader."

Basement said, "Sauron. He's a wizard."

Hired hand said, "Be quiet, Leroy."

I asked, "Where is he now?"

Leroy said, "Walla Walla."

Hired hand said, "Shut up, Leroy."

I put hired hand to sleep.

I said, You're doing good, Leroy. What's Sauron doing in Walla Walla?"

Leroy said, " Jailbreak. He's gonna get us lots of new recruits."

"Great Leroy," I said, "when is he going to do the jailbreak?"

Leroy said, "Already done it."

"OK, Leroy," I said and put him to sleep.

I told the agents I'd put in the house to hang onto Leroy and hired hand and went to Walla Walla.

I looked down on the prison. Flashing lights everywhere and the fences on the north side of the complex were gone. Probably in the Pacific somewhere. There were gaping holes in every building. They weren't from explosions. They were carved out by magic and the pieces had joined the fences.

I dropped to the area of the front door and dropped the invisibility. I flashed my FBI credentials and asked the police captain how many people escaped. He just said, "All of them. They were all gone when we got here.

I went back for another chat with Leroy.

I woke Leroy up and asked him, "Leroy, why were you guarding Mr. Petlock?"

Leroy said, "I was told to make sure he didn't get away or talk to anyone, but don't hurt him."

"What does your boss do on Mr. Petlock's land?"

Leroy said, "We do exercises there and learn teamwork. Me practice with our guns and map reading and scouting for ambushes and like that."

"Leroy, do you a base there?"

"Oh, yeah. Big place underground with electricity and some women who cook for us. Sometimes we get to sleep with them."

"Can you take me to your base?"

"No. I don't know where it is."

"How do you get in or out or there?"

"The boss puts us in a big truck and we drive out the exit and we get where we're going real quick. Same going back to base."

"Leroy, is it always the boss taking you in and out?"

"No, he has Lieutenants and Captains that do it too."

"How many Lieutenants and Captains are there?"

"Let's see. I know two Captains and Four Lieutenants."

"OK. Thanks, Leroy." I put him back to sleep.

I contacted HQ and told them there was an underground base east of my location. I know he didn't build it so it must be either a natural cavern or something built a long time ago. I set them to work to find it.

I was set to go scout the land east of the Petlock ranch when I received a general alert. There was an unseasonable and extreme weather event on Hood Canal. Heavy snowfall, high winds, ice storm, and hail. In spring. I asked for a specific location. The reply was chilling: Bangor Naval Base. It could only mean Sauron was after some Nukes. I ordered every combat wizard to jump in there as soon as possible. Kill the weather magic first, then protect the Nukes, and remove the attackers.

I jumped into the base with my shields raised and reinforced. There was a firefight in progress. I saw more than a hundred bodies on the ground. mostly covered by the heavy snow. It was hard to see the clothing because of the snow. Based on their locations, the attackers were dying in large numbers. That was to be expected. The criminals may have been vicious but they were attacking Marines. Marines were defending from prepared positions they knew like the back of their hands. The Marines had trained and planned for just such an attack. They were outnumbered by the attackers, but that didn't matter. Sauron had thrown his criminal army against the base as a noisy diversion. I felt around with my sense of perception until I found the nuclear weapon storage. Too late.

The military had not planned for an attack by wizards who could teleport through walls. MG had many long discussions with the intelligence agencies of every major country. The decision not to plan for magical attacks was the same in every case. Putting defenses against people with supernormal abilities would leak out. It was likely to be too harmful to the public to reveal that skilled magic users were among them. It was likely to bring the witch trials back into vogue. Instead, the governments took some wizards into the fold to help in 'Special cases.'

There were ten empty positions. The placards identified the missing weapons as W76s. One megaton warheads. They were protected by a PAL (Permissive Arming Link) internally, so it would be hard to set them off. I suspected a technical wizard could find a way to bypass the PAL, given enough time.

The weather died down as soon as Sauron and his cadre left. I guessed they went back to their base in Idaho. I hoped so because that was the only lead we had. I left a small crew to help deal with the mess at Bangor and took most of the team back to the Petlock ranch. Needless to say, all the alphabet agencies had set their hair on fire and were running in circles. I informed HQ I had a lead and needed available manpower to search a large area with a fine toothed comb. We needed to find Sauron and the nukes ASAP. Of course MG had a cordial relationship with most governments. Even though everyone had learned long ago to keep us off the radar. It was how I got my valid FBI credentials. We were offered enough personnel to put ten men in every one of those 50,000 acres. I declined. They wouldn't do much against a wizard of Sauron's caliber.

Chapter 15

I was so scared of losing my whole life I wasn't thinking straight. It took days until I calmed down enough to try getting a vision of Salome. It worked. I could see her perfectly. It was like I was standing beside her. I could hear her and see anything she could see. I spent a lot of time on my cot with my eyes closed, watching her. She was miserable. She would cry herself to sleep at night. She really loved Sauron but he was so caught up in his plans and schemes he didn't have time for her. She was his. She had submitted to him and would only be happy if she was in his presence. She was already the 'obedient wife' even though he only talked work to her.

One day I tuned in to her and she was teaching a group of men how to sense and control objects with the mind. This was what I wanted. I needed to learn more magic to get out of here, and I needed to get out before Sauron returned. She had them practicing with padlocks, showing them how to feel the pins and move them with the mind. Boy, this was perfect. I had a couple of locks I really, really wanted to pick.

She was a good instructor and I picked the lock on my belt before some of the men got their locks open. I relocked it immediately. I needed a plan before I moved. I watched the rest of the class so I didn't miss anything. When it was over I practiced until I could open my belt in two seconds and the door in three. I may not be as good as her, but, boy, was I motivated. I couldn't do anything about the rivets in the shackles and collar. The shackles were too noisy for us to escape unnoticed. I picked up a spool of heavy cord in the kitchen made it invisible and snuck it back into our room. When it was time to escape I would get each girl to use a piece of cord to hold her chain clear of the ground. I looked for some cloth to wrap around the chains, but couldn't find any.

I sat in on every class she gave and I watched her as she moved around the place. I learned the layout and most of all, where the outside doors were. My plan was simple now. Wait until everyone but the night guards were asleep. Open the door to our room and make sure all the women tied up their hobble chain. Go to the kitchen and get a club of some sort. I'd use my invisibility and my shield and fly silently up on the guard at the outside door. Bean him with a rolling pin and open that door. We'd all escape. Once I was outside of the magic shield around the place, I would call in the cavalry.

In two days I had everything in place. Tonight we go. I waited until everyone but the night guards were asleep. I went to all the girls and woke them then gave them the cord and showed them how to get their ankle chains off the ground. I gathered them at the door and briefed them. I showed them how I could fly and turn invisible. Once they had quieted down, I unlocked the door and we crept as quietly as we could to the kitchen. I armed myself with a small skillet and told the others to leave everything. I went invisible, raised my shield and floated up to the guard on the door. I was halfway to him when there came a CLANK from behind me. One of the girls must have dropped her chain on the floor.

The Guard straightened up and turned toward the noise and me. He raised his hand to the alarm button. I raced toward him and was just able to stick my skillet between the alarm button and his hand. His hand hit the invisible barrier. He recoiled with a pained, "That's not supposed to happen" look on his face. I drew back my pan and hit him on the side of his head as he cautiously moved his finger toward the button again.

He dropped like a rock. I unlocked the door and we went outside. I turned off my invisibility so the others could see me. We crept through a short tunnel and we were in the open. I led them into the forest and started trying to reach Bret. Redial for witches. When we got far enough away, I got through and he popped into my vision. He lifted his head immediately and looked at me. I stopped and landed and he said, "Don't move. I'm coming to you."

I opened my eyes and he was there in front of me. He pulled me to him and we kissed so long I was afraid we would be discovered. When we broke for air we were surrounded by a lot of very grim faced men. They were itching for a fight.

He examined my collar and I knew he was going to get rid of it. I said, "Wait, leave it for now." I couldn't explain it but I wanted him to see me as a slave for a moment.

He said, "I can remove it and your shackles now."

I looked at him and kissed him again. I said, "I want to wear them for you, Just for a little while. I'll tell you why when we're in bed. You can remove them when we're both home. They don't stop me from doing anything. OK?"

He just shook his head, but he left them on me. Just for a little while I wanted to play bondage games with him in the bedroom. I wondered if it really made sex better.

I showed him the chastity belt and said, "Its OK to get rid of this, Bret."

He dematerialized it. I've got to learn how to do that. And teleport. And make things. And an endless list of skills. He or one of the others did the same for the rest of my friends. I told him the other women had them too and theirs dropped away, shocking them. I was afraid Bret would get too angry to fight well, but he seemed calm. His training I guess.

Bret sent the other women with me to HQ.

He asked, "Can you show me the entrance to his base?"

"Sure," I said, "its right down here. I took off and he and all the troops followed me. I showed him the entrance to the base. He sent his troops in to pacify it. I had one burning question for him, "Do you know who this creep is? He kidnapped me and put me in his harem."

Bret smiled and said, "He calls himself 'Sauron' after the evil wizard in the Lord of the Rings. He's pretty tough but I think my training gives me an edge. I intend to catch him. He used his army of criminals to steal ten nuclear warheads and everyone is looking for him. I'm going to send you to HQ. You can talk to Gus and Millie from there, but don't leave until I get back. Sauron's going to want to get his harem back. Hey, maybe he'd trade the nukes for you?"

I smacked him in the chest. "You rat fink. Don't even joke about that."

He pulled me to him and we repeated the kiss. It lasted a long time. When we broke he said. "I have an apartment at HQ. Why don't you stay there until I can get back."

I wanted to stay with him, but he was right. I was no good in a fight and he'd have to protect me.

I said, "OK. Hurry back. I love you," and I was in his apartment in HQ.

I followed my team into the underground base. It was bigger than I expected. We spread out and found thirty five men sleeping so we reinforced their sleep and sent them to HQ to be sorted out. We found forty women, some locals and some from the Philippines. Shackled and locked up. They went to HQ also. We found one woman, not shackled, in a nice bedroom.

She said her name was Salome and she was Sauron's Assistant. She went to a different location in HQ, under guard. I blocked her powers, otherwise she would just have teleported out.

We waited for Sauron and his wizards to appear. I was surprised he hadn't shown up here immediately after the theft of the warheads. I guess he's not bringing them here. Nonetheless, I was sure he would come here eventually. His women, his assistant, and his non-magical troops were here.

Chapter 16

It was the wee hours of the morning when I got to HQ. Bret had sent me to his apartment. I brushed my teeth with his toothbrush. I wouldn't think of sharing a toothbrush before this. When I saw it a devilish mirth grabbed me and by the time I finished, I felt like I had been kissing him.

I threw that ugly burlap bag in the trash. I never wanted to feel burlap again. I found a nightgown and some women's clothes in a closet. I needed to talk to Bret about that, too.

I slid under his covers and smelled him. I fondled the covers and drifted in his scent. I had never known a sheet could be sexy, but it was. I felt wonderful. It was so, so, great to be free of that damned belt. I still wore the collar and shackles, but now they were Bret's, not Sauron's. I was free to move everything. Free to touch all of my body. But mostly I was free of the hold Sauron had on me. As I was nearly asleep I felt Lucifer join me on the bed. I said, "Goodnight, Lucifer." He purred softly and I fell asleep.

I woke as Bret slid into the bed beside me. I rolled toward him and ran my hands all over him. Every part of him was hard, and I mean every part. We kissed for a heavenly moment.

He said, "You were going to tell me why you wanted to keep the collar and shackles?"

"When I first saw you, I recognized you. Not as a person, but as a concept. When I was old enough to be interested in boys, I discovered the Conan books by Robert E. Howard. I was enthralled. Conan was bog, tough fast and an instinctive leader. That was you. I used to go to sleep dreaming of being Conan's slave girl. Of helping him conquer the world from below. I was less than the dirt beneath his sandals. And I loved him as only a teenage girl can love a hero. I've come know you since that first time. You are the hero that I worshipped. I want to wear your chains and love you better than any other woman could. Your touch makes me swoon. I've read that bondage improves sex. I want to try that. I've read that spanking or whipping a girl's bottom makes for better sex. I want that too. Most of all I want you to have the best experience of your life when you take me. Chain me, take me, own me, Master."

He threw the covers back and rolled me on my back. I couldn't spread my ankles very far now. He noticed and said, "Pull your feet up to your bottom then spread your knees."

I said, "Yes sir. I think your slave's wrists need some attention, sir."

He said, "Good of you to remind me. He held my wrists in front of me and steel bands grasped my wrists. He pulled them over my head and they fastened themselves to my collar. I was completely helpless, but no more so than I wanted to be. For me, his chains, and cuffs did not make me feel vulnerable, they make me feel safe. My body was bound, but my mind was free and my soul sang.

He stroked my body and I responded rapidly. My arousal swelled and before I knew it I had a huge orgasm. He continued rubbing all over me and I was thrown into orgasm three times before he deigned to enter me. I couldn't move. I relished his absolute mastery and control. I was spent, exhausted, and so happy when he left me. He took off all my bonds and left me curled beside him in the bed. I slept the sleep of the well fucked girl.

I woke up alone and famished but all I could find in the apartment was beer and cheese. I found a note. He thanked me for an unforgettable day. Told me he had saved my toys, and said he had to go back to Idaho and would be back midday. I showered and put on the clothes I found in the closet. I looked at slacks and panties. I chose the longest skirt I could find which was still quite short. They were a good fit, though a little too thin and short to be considered work attire. At least I had some idea of what clothes Bret would like to see me wear.

I went to the cafeteria and got some yogurt and an orange. After I gobbled those down, I got a cup of strong coffee to go and went looking for Esmerelda. I didn't care about much at this time besides my crystal clear certainty I wanted Bret. I was going to wrench him away from her no matter what it took and I didn't care what he or she thought about it. I wanted a showdown. I marched into her office and sat in her visitor's chair. Lucifer joined me.

She said, "Hi, Suzanne. I hear you had quite an ordeal. I'm glad you're OK."

I said, "Me too. I had quite a while to think while I was being held prisoner by that gang. One of the things I'm quite certain of now is that I consider Bret my boyfriend and we need to talk."

I expected a blowup and showdown now. Instead she positively beamed at me. She said, "Suzanne, that's wonderful. I've been hoping the big lug would find someone to take care of him. I'm happy for both of you."

"You are? I thought you and he..."

"Don't be absurd. He's my brother. We lived together for way too many years."

"Brother? But I thought..."

"Wrong-O, Suzy. I hereby bequeath all my interest in him to you. Keep him happy."

I couldn't believe my ears. All my worrying was for nothing. I should have cleared up their relationship at our first talk. I was so happy. I had feared we would be rivals, enemies as only women can be. Instead, we might be friends. I asked, "Esmerelda, I like Bret a lot. Do you have any recommendations for things I should avoid or do?"

She looked thoughtful. Finally, she said, "Bret is Determined and practical. He likes to argue fine points. He'd probably make a good lawyer. But he wants good opinions. Don't back down from an argument if you think you're right. He likes a fighter. In bed, I don't know, but I've heard he can play rough or soft depending on what you like. Oh, and he doesn't like clingy women. Stand on your own two feet when he's away and make him respect what you do when he's around. He has to jump out of town on a moment's notice and he'll expect you to understand that. And take care of business when he's gone. On the other hand, there's no one else you want at your back when the chips are down."

"OK," I said, "your advice is to be a partner, not a dependent."

"Right on, Suzy," she said.

"I'd like to help him with this bad guy he's chasing. Not just to help him win, but also because the creep kidnapped me and put me in his harem. I want to help take him down. Do you know anything about this wizard. He calls himself "Sauron" from the Lord of the Rings.

Esmerelda said, "Well, Sauron's real name is Bart Maverick Thorne."

I was flabbergasted. He was Bret's evil twin? I said, "He's Bret's evil twin?" She grinned, "Yep, and my brother too. You can tell from their names that our mother is a big fan of "Maverick" the TV show."

"When did Bart turn evil wizard?"

She said, " it was a gradual thing. Bart never did have much use for rules and never learned to play nice with others. He and Bret are extremely competitive. He went into the world to 'Make his fortune' when he was seventeen. He's been a pain in everyone's ass ever since. When he learned Bret joined MG as a sort of wizard policeman, Bart became a criminal. He's a powerful wizard so he's immune to everyone except MG. Its extremely difficult to catch a teleporting wizard."

"Wow. This may be harder than I thought. What can you tell me about Bart as a junior wizard."

She looked up and to her right as she thought. She said, "Its been a long time. Bart was the artistic, romantic one. Bret was more left brain. Bart is a pretty good artist, he plays a fair piano. He had girlfriends from ten until he left. He changed them often. He's less controlled than Bret, gets mad easily and cools off quickly. Mercurial, I'd say. I remember their biggest arguments were over the worth of people without talents. Bart thought they were a waste of oxygen. Bret pointed out that they were pretty smart sometimes. They often used their brains better than talents that could use magic. That's all I can think of now. You should stay away from him. He's powerful and he wants you."

"OK, " I said, "he's creative, powerful, ruthless, and it seems he wants a lot of money."

She looked puzzled, "Money?"

"Yeah. Bret said he had stolen ten nuclear warheads. Only two reasons for that. Sell them for a lot of money, or send a message in a big voice. I'm hoping its money he wants."

We were both silent with our thoughts for a while. Then I said, I have a glimmer of a plan. I have a magic ring. Do you think its strong enough to affect Bart? If so, maybe I can redirect his energy and provide some protection for myself if he comes calling again."

She said, I'm not sure. Both he and Bret are quite powerful among wizards. Generally, it takes a powerful enchantment to affect a powerful wizard. Your ring may be powerful enough or not. You won't know until you try it. Have you tried it on a witch or wizard?

"No, I didn't think about it when I was a captive. And I didn't know anyone with a talent before that. It works fine on untalented folk. Hey, Salome. You've got her here don't you. She wants Bart to love her. I could try it on her and see if it has any effect. If it works I can change her back."

Esmerelda said, "That's a good idea. Let's go see her. She's in detention. She's still a witch, but Bret damped her power so she can't escape. How does the ring work?"

"Simple, I just make a simple rhyme that affects their love in some way and they do it."

"So you need a rhyme to make her fall out of love with Bart and if she's still in love with him, it didn't work?"

"Right. Now I need a rhyme. Oh, and they don't have to hear the rhyme."

"OK, she said, "how about: You think you love Sauron, but now that's gone."

"That's great. I need to see her when I say it. Then we can go ask how she feels about him."

She led me down into a sub basement and had the guard bring Salome to an interview room. She was still wearing her black leather cat suit. We looked at her through the one way glass and I recited the ditty. Then we went in to talk to her.

I spoke first and said, "Hi Salome. Remember me?"

She looked up and smiled, "You're Suzy. I'm sorry you went through that. If I could have I would have traded places with you."

"I know."

Lucifer jumped into my lap. Salome said, "Wow. You have a familiar. You are a witch. No wonder you escaped. I always wanted a familiar but none ever found me."

I asked, "They have to find you? I never knew. Lucifer was my mother's then he adopted me. This is Esmerelda. She's Sauron's sister."

"Wow, his sister. I never thought of him as having family. He never spoke of you."

Esmerelda said, "I'm sure. He's been away from the family for about ten years. By the way, his given name is Bart Thorne. Suzanne tells me you're in love with him. Is that true?"

Salome said, "Yes. I've been in love with him since we met. I don't think he knows I'm even a woman." Her voice grew cold, "I'm his assistant."

Esmerelda said, "Well, there's always hope. Is there anything you need?"

Salome asked, "Could I have something to read?"

Esmerelda said, "Surely. I'll have a selection sent in. Goodbye."

We left and told the guard we were finished. She asked him to send a selection of fiction books in to her.

We went back to the lounge and sat down. I said, "that didn't work. Do you know of any way to strengthen an enchanted ring?"

She said, "Yes. Its done exactly the same way you place the enchantment in the first place. The stronger the enchantment power, the stronger the spell. We can make it stronger by getting more witches and wizards to add to the spell. It should be done all at once for the best results. I'll call a general meeting tomorrow morning and ask everyone to pile on. Your ring should become more powerful. Then we can test it on Salome again."

Esmerelda put out a call for an emergency meeting tomorrow morning. She asked for all talents not urgently needed elsewhere to join us in the auditorium.

We ate lunch together in the cafeteria. Good, plain food.

"Esmerelda, are there some witches with visions like mine I can talk to?"

She looked thoughtful, "Suzy, I've never heard of anyone that uses visions like yours. I'll ask Marcus. He's our head librarian."

"OK. I hope he has something. I want to improve my visions to be more useful. I'd like to talk to someone else who uses them."

She asked, "Tomorrow we're going to try and strengthen your ring so you can use it against Bart. If we're successful, what do you want to do with him. He's still my brother and he's got some good in him."

"I don't want to hurt him. I want some defense so he can't just snatch me again so easily. Ideally, I'd like to be able to find the nukes and get him to give up his life of crime. Probably wishful thinking."

Esmerelda said, "You need to see him and say a rhyme. It needs to be short and ready to go. What about just putting him to sleep? Something like, "Bart is a creep , he's fast asleep."

"That's perfect. You'd make a good witch."

She laughed and said, "Pretty bad poetry, though."

"Yeah, but no ones going to hear it but me."

I went back to Bret's apartment and sat in an easy chair. I leaned back and thought about Bret. His picture came up at once. "Shiny. This beats cell phones every way possible. Any sign of Sauron? By the way, Esmerelda says he's your evil twin."

Bret laughed and said, "I guess you could call him that. Evil is a little strong. I like to think of him as my headstrong, self assured, greedy and antagonistic twin."

I laughed, "Oh, that is so much better than evil twin. I'm relieved. So, any sign of your headstrong, self assured, greed and antagonistic twin?"

"Nope. I hoped he'd bring the nukes here, but he must have a more secure site elsewhere. Since Esme is telling you about our black sheep, you two must be getting on well?"

"Oh yes, we've gotten close enough to start being co-conspirators."

"Oh my. This may be bad. What kind of conspiracy are you working on?

"You'll like this. We have a plan to strengthen my magic love ring. If it works and it gets strong enough, I will use it to put Sauron asleep."

Bret looked worried, "Good idea, but don't you have to see your target before the ring works?"

'Now I was worried too and said, But I can be a long ways off and he doesn't have to see me or hear me."

Bret said, Yes, but remember the part about you have to see him? If you can see him, he will see and feel you. That's too close for safety, Suzy. His reach is longer than you can imagine."

Well, Bret, darling, you will have to protect me long enough for me to say my rhyme and its short. Say, maybe I can just see him in a vision?"

"That's worse. If you can see him in a vision, he can see you and teleport to you. Remember how I came to you at home? Normal eyesight is much safer."

"Bret, how about a CCTV or video. If you had one and I could see him, then he couldn't see me and I'd be far away."

"Yeah, that might work. I don't know about your ring's limits so its a guess. Can you test it in HQ? You try and bulk up the ring and I'll set up a video link from here to HQ right now in case it does work."

"When are you coming home? I miss you."

"If Bart doesn't show up here this afternoon, I'll be back by five. Would you like to have a nice dinner somewhere new?"

"Anywhere with you, lover."

"Bye."

"Bye." And I broke the connection.

Chapter 17

I wonder, can I reach Esmerelda this way too? I closed my eyes again and thought of her. A vision popped into being. She was at a desk looking down. She looked up and said, Your communications are working I see.

"Look like. I was talking to Bret and he would like me to see if my hex works when I can see my target over a video link. Is there someone here who can help me get a video link to someone who's not a talent?"

Of course. You just want to test your ability? You can't harm or embarrass the contact. OK."

Of course not."

"OK. Come to my office in a half hour and I can be ready to help you."

"OK." I broke the connection and thought about the test. I wanted the person on the other end to do something innocuous and unusual. I know. I'll have the person touch their chin. I'd say, "I don't know where you've been, with your finger touch your chin."

"Boy," I thought, " Its a good thing these rhymes don't have to be heard by anyone. It would be embarrassing."

I had a half hour to wait so I called the office. Millie answered, "Boss, are you OK?

"Hi Millie, Yes, I'm fine. I escaped and the good guys came and cleaned out the rats nest. How's Gus?"

"He's been unbearable since you disappeared. He's like an angry lion. He's working off his anger by finding some of your skips. Here he is."

"Gus said, "Suzy? You're OK?"

"Hi Gus. Yeah, I'm OK and safe and bad guys are on the run. Millie says you're finding some skips?"

"Yeah, sorry, "he said, "I was angry and bored and I figured I'd keep busy until you got back. Remember how you said you needed a helicopter? "

"That's right, Gus. You can fly and turn invisible. How do you find them to start with?"

"I don't have your gift of visions so I start with my investigative skills. Its easy to stake out a place when you're invisible. And following a skip is no problem when you can fly. Once I spot them they're dead meat. Say, Why don't you do bail bonds, then I can just fly them to jail without having to meet an agent. I could be your agent."

"Maybe. It sounds like a good idea. I'll need to find some startup cash. But my friends will help, I'm sure. Who have you brought in?"

"John Atkins and Sonny Johnstone."

Assault 3rd and Possession with intent to distribute, I knew.

"Was it fun?"

"My gosh, Suzy. It was a blast. Flying. Me. It was like a dream. I don't know how to describe it. Its like being Superman."

I asked, "Did you have any trouble flying?"

"Nah. I had a midair collision with a seagull. It was his fault. He turned right in front of me. Didn't hurt him. He flew away. I saw a guy looking up at the crazy bird. I was glad he couldn't see me.

"Just remember you're not invulnerable, OK , Gus"

"Yeah. Spoilsport. I'll be careful. Glad you're OK, Suzy."

"Bye Gus."

I still had twenty minutes until seeing Esmerelda. I went exploring. I had seen the "jail" where Salome was housed. I had seen Bret's apartment, a cafeteria and a gym. I looked into classrooms, and medical facility, and a couple of laboratories. Then my time was up and I went to Esmerelda's office. Lucifer was on a chair waiting for me. Damn, he's good.

She had a computer running SKYPE set up and a woman was on the screen. She said, "Just a minute," and muted the call.

Esmerelda looked at me and said, "This is Jenny, a friend. What are you going to tell her to do?"

I plan to say, "I don't know where you've been, with your finger touch your chin."

Esmerelda said, "OK that's innocuous enough. I'll open the call and you get off to the side so she can't see you then say it softly and if it works, she'll touch her chin."

"Let's do it."

She started the conversation again. They were talking about Jenny's children. I said my spell and it worked. Jenny touched her chin as she was speaking. Esmerelda ended the call gracefully and turned off the computer.

She said, "Planning on zapping Bart through a camera huh?"

"Yes. Bret thinks it will be too dangerous for me to get close to him."

"He's probably right. Bart is an excellent wizard, fast and powerful. So is Bret but they're so evenly matched bystanders can get hurt."

I said, "I'll let Bret know that the remote spell works. The next question is whether we can pump up the juice enough to affect Bart. I'll see you in the morning then, 'bye.

I went back to Bret's apartment. He could be back any time and I wanted to be there to greet him. I thought he might be tired after being out all night and I wanted to soothe his aching body, so to speak.

I put on a t-shirt and shorts and read the NY Times found on a counter. A day old, but crammed with interesting stuff I hadn't seen before. Lucifer sat in my lap and purred. He was good company, but I missed Bret.

I was lost in an article when Lucifer jumped off the couch and I felt his hands touch my shoulders. I sprang up and bounded over the couch like a kangaroo. He caught me as I reached him and pulled me close. He held me and said, "That's the kind of enthusiasm that'll get you into bed without any dinner."

"Suits me. I've missed you, ya big lunk."

I was engulfed in his arms and once again dwarfed by his assurance and presence. He was tremendous in every way imaginable. I nuzzled his shoulder. He tasted of salt and sweat. Of heat and desire. I raised my head and devoured him with my eyes.

I licked my lips and asked, "Do you still have that sleeping mask?"

"Of course, Suzy. I never leave home without it."

He held me with one hand and dangled the mask from his other hand. "Now?"

"Definitely now."

He carried me into the bedroom, flexed his magic muscles, and our clothes were laying on a chair. He stood me on the floor and handed me the mask. I slipped it on and flopped back on the bed. I put my hands behind my head and interlaced my fingers. I drew my feet up close to my ass and spread my legs as wide as possible. I was hot and wanted to be as open as possible for him to touch me everywhere. His bare skin touched mine and I burned all over. I felt the heat radiating from my belly He said, "Just feel."

He sat on the bed beside me and rubbed oil into my skin. Just a light coat and he massaged it into every inch of my body. I was getting frantic. His rubbing was exciting me and making me highly aroused. He was turning every inch of my body into an erogenous zone. No matter where he touched me my nerves flamed and shouted to my mind. At last he played with my breasts. He kneaded them and rolled my nipples between his fingers. He was gentle, but as my nipples hardened , they were right on the edge of pain. He patted the outside of my breasts, lightly with his hands, left, right, left, right. I flamed into an enormous orgasm. My body jumped and twisted. I felt my belly spasm ferociously. My shoulders and bottom came off the bed and my belly spasmed again and again. As soon as I relaxed he put a hand to my loins and started stroking my labia. They swelled instantly and soon were spreading themselves in invitation. He stroked my inner lips and I was soon panting my need. My belly spasmed over and over and my love juices flowed into my needy lips. He slid his fingers out from between my nether lips and painted my fragrant juice on my lips. I opened my mouth and he thrust his moist fingers into my mouth. I sucked them clean and he stroked my brow.

"Bret, Sir, please take me. I need you in me. Please take me, I beg you."

He stroked my pussy, lightly with his huge hand. I climaxed as soon as his hand touched me. I bucked and screamed, "YES. Oh yes." I moaned my pleasure and he kept rubbing, stimulating me. I was so helpless in his grip. I couldn't move any way except to spasm and buck in my passion. I was a tightly coiled ball of heat rapidly growing hotter. His hands were merciless and so incredibly effective.

I climaxed again. I was lost in my heat. I had no control. He was a master playing me like an instrument. I squealed, I pled, I writhed under his hands. I couldn't stop climaxing. Finally, he climbed on me and we merged. I was wonderfully stretched and filled. He pumped a few times, each one driving me higher until we came together. His hot sperm flooding into me in the greatest ecstasy I had ever known. I screamed with joy and love and everything went black.

I was only out a moment. I was aware of his hot, hard, wonderful body pressing me into the bed. He was still in me, and I felt him softening, getting smaller. I separated my hands and put my arms around his neck. I pulled his head down onto mine and we kissed. Not the hard passionate kiss when he returned. We kissed softly and just as passionately. I was so frigging happy he was here and I didn't want him to leave me yet. I like hosting his soft hot cock in my love canal. I thought this would be a fine, fine way to wake and start the day. I wrapped my legs around his and rubbed my feet up and down his legs. They were hard with corded muscle. It was like rubbing a smooth tree trunk. I hope he was proud of his body because I sure was. He was like a Greek God, hard in all the right places and soft in me.

He was a master lover and knew just how to play my body for maximum pleasure. This was as good as the first time we made love. He used one hand and gently slid the sleeping mask over my head. I opened my eyes and looked into his icy blue eyes above mine. He ran his tongue over my lips and I almost fainted again. Was there anything he did that didn't heat me up?

He asked, gently, "Do you want to go out for dinner, still?"

I whispered, " You need to get up before I can think again, my sweet wizard."

I felt his weight pressing me down decrease more and more. Until I was hanging from his floating body by my arms and legs. Then my weight decreased until I was effortlessly clinging to him. I was flying up into him. He was still in me. We were like two eagles, mating in air.

"Can you think now, my sexy witch?"

"Less than ever. Was your father an eagle?"

He laughed and said, "No, he's a rock." He pulled out and set me on the floor.

I didn't resist, but I didn't want to be apart from him. I wanted this evening to be memorable and end just like we started it. I said, "I want to wear elegant clothes and dine in style in a memorable place. Then I want you to take me back to bed and show me how to make love in the air."

I'd never seem such big grin on his face. He just said, "Done. Let's take a shower and I'll dress you in elegance."

The shower was fun too. He opened the door to the bath and it was not the one I had used two hours ago. It was bigger than the rest of his apartment. I whistled and said, "This wasn't here before."

He smirked and said, "Wizard."

We passed the toilet, bidet, jacuzzi and sauna to reach the shower. There was no door. There was a curving tiled wall with six shower nozzles, three high, three low. The top three had wands. The outer wall was glass tiles and warm sunshine was flooding through them. I asked, "How..."

He just said, "Magic."

Our shower was almost as much fun as sex. The jets of water flowed out of the nozzles and curved in air to gently warm and caress my skin everywhere at once. The very air seemed magical. I was like Alice when she went down the rabbit hole. It was such a wondrous, enchanted feeling. I hated to stop, but I was getting hungry. I said, "Food now, please."

The water stopped and he got a big fluffy towel and dried me. He was gentle but firm. His touch made me flame with passion again. I watched him and thought about the future.

Before we had ever had sex I was powerful. I had made the decision to let him enter me. I wanted him so bad. Now that we had made love, no matter how many times, he had the power. He could decide to love me again or leave. I had submitted to him and given him my power. The only way I would ever have power over him would be if he decided to stay faithful to me. Now, I wasn't sure I wanted that level of commitment for either of us. That commitment would changes us, would twist our relationship in ways we couldn't predict. I don't think any woman could tame the master who had guided me to the strongest orgasms I had ever felt. I wanted him to keep all my power and use it on me whenever he wanted. I would endure whatever it took to stay faithful to him, but I couldn't ask it of him. He was too magnificent just the way he was.

I looked up at him and said, "That shower was almost as mind blowing as the sex, Master Wizard. Every time we play together it gets better. Is it possible practice is improving your touch?"

He looked thoughtful and said, "You may be right. I seem to get new ideas whenever we're together. I may need more practice to reach my full potential. But now let's get dressed."

He said, I usually undress ladies. If you don't like something, yell."

"OK."

He materialized an expensive black tuxedo on himself and said, "Men's clothes are simple. I've got to think about yours. Its a shame to hide such a great birthday suit, though."

"Get on with it, lover." I stood there in my birthday suit as he worked his magic. I felt a tingle then a slight pressure in my loins. I looked down and he had put a small clamp at the top of my clit. small silver chains supporting three turquoise beads dangled almost three inches down from it. I looked sexy as hell. He asked, "Like it.? I've heard its stimulating to wear."

I said, "This wasn't what I had in mind, but it is stimulating. Go ahead."

The felt his ghostly touch on my chest. I looked down again. I wore a fine silver necklace with an intricate pattern of silver and diamonds . It continued down and split into two chains that went below my breasts then curved back up to my nipples. Each nipple had a snug silver, diamond encrusted disc around it. The chain fastened to the bottom of the disc.

He asked, "Well?"

I liked the effect. I said, "Nice. Go on."

He put shiny blue silk thong and a half bra. My nipples and their jewelry were highlighted. "You've got to cover them up now," I said.

Shoes came next, Dark blue Manolo Blahnik pumps with a diamond buckle and 2.75 inch heels. Now I felt pampered.

Finally he put a blue evening strapless gown of satin and lace with a deep neckline and a full skirt on me. He turned me to face the mirror. I looked like I was at the Academy Awards ceremony. He had even made my hair shiny and smooth. I was almost ready for my debut. I looked at my face. I needed makeup.

Bret said, Just a minute. He went to Lucifer and said, "Lucifer, I'm going to take Suzy to dinner. I'll watch out for her so you can go play until morning." Lucifer jumped off the chair and ran out of the room..

He said, "I've made arrangements." He transported us to a beauty salon somewhere they spoke French. He conversed with the women and they worked on my face for twenty minutes. I looked like a movie star, or at least a model. I walked out to the front of the salon.

He looked at me and said, "You look like why the riot started. Lovely. Shall we go to dinner, Love?"

I nodded, afraid to speak.

He transported us to an expensive looking restaurant. I saw a view through large windows of a big city seen from above. There were large yellow and red flowers in elegant vases. "Where are we," I asked?

He said, "This is the Lung King Heen restaurant in Hong Kong. The name means 'View of the Dragon.' It has excellent Cantonese cuisine. It's the first Chinese restaurant in the world to receive three Michelin stars. Do you like to dance?"

"Yes, very much," I said, "Is there a dance floor here?"

"Of course," he said, "we'll try it out after dinner."

I had scallops and a salad, of course it had French names I couldn't pronounce. He had duck. They were, of course, excellent. We were overdressed compared to the other patrons, but we shone like emeralds in a sea of sand. Everyone looked at us and I felt like I was the star of the show. I saw a couple of women eye my necklace and smile when they saw it descended down into my dress. I felt risque and worldly, far beyond average. If only they knew.

The dance floor was half full and they were doing a salsa series. I had taken a few classes in salsa but didn't get to practice. Bret could have taught the classes. He was naturally athletic and made the dance look so easy. He coached me mentally and I improved a lot. It was fun exercise. Every time I took a step that insidious little clamp on my clit brushed on my most sensitive erogenous zone. After a half hour of dancing I was ready to rip my clothes off and jump in bed again. When the dance ended I whispered in his ear, "Hey big boy, ready for dessert?"

He led me out the door onto a terrace. When no one was looking he made us both invisible and lifted us off into the clear sky and out over Hong Kong harbor. We floated gently for a while, just holding hands and admiring the view.

We kissed and I felt my clothes slithering off my body. His too, apparently since we were soon skin to skin. In the air, a thousand feet over Hong Kong. His arms were around me, but we were both floating. I felt ghostly fingers all over my body, stroking, pinching my nipples, making me boil. I spread my legs and he slid closer. His member gently prodded at my entrance. My labia engorged and spread open for him, inviting him in. I was sprinkling the harbor with my love juices. He slid in with that slippery friction that made me boil even more. Bret was the most patient, in control, lover I could imagine. I gasped and moaned through three huge orgasms before he came in me. He filled me with his hot spend And I orgasmed yet again. The biggest and best yet. I know my screams of pleasure were heard all over the waterfront. I heard laughter and applause from below and I didn't care. When I had calmed he transported us back to his bedroom, still in me, and we lay on the bed for a while.

"Another shower," he asked?

"I said, "No thanks. I'm too tired and content just the way I am."

He pulled out and lay beside me. We went to sleep on top of the covers.

I woke up laying on my side with Bret wrapped around me spoon like. It was amazingly comfortable. My head was resting on his bicep. A soft rock and bigger than my head. I could tell from his breathing he was awake. "Morning, my hero. Are you ready to face the world?"

He said, "I guess its time. Esme says they'll be ready for you in an hour."

"Oh," I asked, "I didn't hear the phone."

Of course, he doesn't use phones unless he has to. He just said, "Wizard."

I showered and dressed. We ate breakfast in the cafeteria and went to the auditorium. It was full of people of all ages, sizes, shapes and disposition. Bret led me to the front and we sat on the stage with Esmerelda. Lucifer sat at my feet.

She went to a microphone and said, "Thanks for coming. You all know Bret and this is Suzanne Ryder. She has a talent and only recently discovered us. Of course she's a witch but has only received a little training so far. She came into possession of a ring, apparently enchanted by Asmodeus. It isn't strong enough to affect people with a talent. You also know that Bart Thorne, my brother, is a powerful wizard and has been causing trouble for some time. We have a plan to strengthen Suzanne's ring with your help. So it is strong enough to control Bart without killing him. As you know we can strengthen an enchantment through adding on the power of morel talents. It should last for two or three spells, long enough to redirect Bart. The process is simple, exactly the same that we use on our refugee feeding program. An empowered person focuses on a an object. We use a metal bowl for food, here its her ring. We picture some food, or in this case love and envision it in the object. In a bowl, we can feed a person for a week on one charge. Here we hope to make it strong enough to affect a powerful wizard."

" Suzy, hold up the ring please."

I held up my hand, fingers spread.

"Now everyone concentrate on love flowing into the ring."

I felt the ring grow warm and swell and suddenly I felt a sharp pain in my chest. I clutched both hands to my breasts and fainted.

Part 4 : Instructions

Chapter 18

I woke up in Bret's bed with Esmerelda, Bret and a man I didn't know standing over me. Lucifer was lying on the pillow beside me. The man was feeling my pulse. Bret said, "She's awake Doc."

The Doctor looked at me and asked, "How do you feel now Ms. Ryder."

I let my mind wander around my body. I feel pretty good Doctor. My breasts hurt a little like I've been stuck with a pin. Not a lot, but its there. More of a discomfort than a pain.

"I'd like to examine you, if I may. Bret, Esme, would you wait in the living room for a minute?

They left and closed the door.

"Can you sit up," the Doctor asked? "By the way," he said, I'm Alex Walker, the head physician at the MG medical facility."

"Glad to meet you Doctor. Did they tell you what happened?"

"I was in the room, trying to aid your project, so I know it all. Nothing we were doing should have had the effect on you I saw. The ring must have had some sort of protection spell built in. Would you take off your to, please?"

I did as he asked. He looked around a little and said, "Now the bra, please."

I unhooked it and slid it over my arms and I felt something drag on my nipples. I looked down at them just as he said, "My, my."

Big, frigging gold rings. One in each breast. Just behind the nipple. Heavy, two inches in diameter, a quarter inch thick, gold. The one in my left breast had the word "LOVE" engraved in its front in big, capital, letters. The one in my right breast had the word "LUST." I held up my hand and looked at the Love Ring. It was gone.

The Doctor said, "you don't seem to have a medical condition. I'm going to call the others back. They need to see this. It lies in their areas of specialty."

I said, "OK, Doc. Call them."

Esmerelda said, "Oh my goodness."

Bret said, "Looks like you strengthened the ring, Suzy. Are they tender?"

"Yes, you idiot. I was just impaled by a pound of gold, " I snapped.

He said, Doc, can you heal the nipples?"

The Doctor said, "Sure, It'll just take a moment." He reached out and lifted each breast in a hand and closed his eyes. Magically they felt better. He released my boobs and, except for the weight of the metal, they felt normal."

"I said, "Wow, Doc. That's much better. How do you do that?"

He said, "I imagine its just like how you do your visions, Suzy. I've got to go. I've got another patient." He left.

I felt stirrings in my loins. Oh No. I grabbed my blouse and held it up in front of me. I was about to orgasm. Guys, could you leave me alone for a minute, please. Now. They scuttled out of the room just in time. As soon as they turned away from me I started to cool down. I took a few deep breaths. I felt fine again. Now what?

Bret called through the door, Suzy, are you OK?"

I yelled back, "I'm fine. Bret could you come in here?"

He came in and closed the door. He looked at me and I started becoming aroused. I asked, sweetly, "Bret, honey, would you mind turning around, please?"

He turned around and I felt normal again. Great. I said, "It seems that the rings make me horny whenever you look at me."

Bret said, smugly, "I have that effect on many girls, even those without magic love rings."

Bastard. "No," I said, "I like you to look at me, but now, if you do, I start getting aroused. I'm afraid I'll dissolve into an orgasm in a minute. I won't be able to do anything if I'm always coming."

Reasonably, Bret asked, "If you get aroused, do you always wind up with an orgasm?"

Hmmm. "No," I said, "not always."

"OK," he said, "let's see how long or if you get an orgasm." He turned around and looked at me. My arousal spiked up. I wanted to grab him and kiss him, but I held back, just like I would if we were in a meeting or something. I was having a little trouble concentrating, but I think I was managing it.

"So, Suzy," he said, "tell me about your business. How many employees do you have?"

I saw what he was doing. A little test of my concentration. I said, "I have two employees. Gus and Millie. Millie is my office manager and receptionist. Gus is my strong right hand. He's lethal and I take him with me when I go in the field and there's some danger. And of course there's Lucifer, but I only pay him with cat food and all the mice he can find."

He asked, "Are you stable or is your arousal increasing?"

"I'm stable and I want you a lot."

"Good," he said, "I'm going to have Esme change places with me. Remember your reactions."

He called Esme in and left us alone. I explained what was going on.

Esme asked, "How do you feel?"

"Horny as hell," I said.

Is it a general need for sex, a desire for Bret, or do you want me now?"

I thought about my feelings. I said, "You're right. I wanted Bret when he was here. Now I want you. These rings are turning me into a slut."

She said, "not your fault. Can I try something?"

"What?"

She said, "I want to touch your rings and see what happens."

"What do you think will happen?"

"I don't know, but it seems that it could either give you an orgasm or stop the arousal. Or nothing."

"OK, I said, I lifted my blouse and she touched one of the rings. I orgasmed, spectacularly and noisily. Esme didn't notice because she orgasmed at the same time. Also noisily.

Bret sprang through the door and found both of us writhing and moaning in our orgasms. He smiled and asked, "Have my girls been experimenting with the rings? It looks like you found an unexpected feature of them."

When I could speak again, I said, "She touched a ring."

Esme said, "And a mighty fine ring you have there. I'd like to touch it again. When I've recovered. That was a fine orgasm."

Bret said, "Suzy, you know the power in an enchanted object is used up when you use it. I have no idea how much you have left, but you should probably save the fun for after you've zapped Bart. And Esme, You and Suzy need to try her enhanced rings on Salome. If it works, I've got the video set up between here and the reservoir. The techs are putting the receiver in your office Esme. Its just temporary."

Esmerelda said, "Fine. We'll test it on Salome now and let you know how it works. I'm going to get Jason to start teaching Suzy how to teleport. It'll make her a lot safer and more flexible if she helps us again."

He said, "Good idea. I'm going back to Idaho. Keep me informed. Bye." And he was gone.

I put on my bra and blouse then Esme and I went to see Salome. I decided to use the touch the chin rhyme so it wouldn't cause any long term effect. We sat in the same room as before and Esme engaged Salome in a discussion about where we might look for Bart. Every time Salome looked at me I felt arousal. I fought to keep my features neutral and I said the rhyme to myself. It worked. Salome touched her chin . Esme saw it too and we ended the interview.

We went back to Esme's office and found the video receiver. I used my vision to talk to Bret. I sat in her guest chair and Lucifer landed in my lap. I closed my eyes and thought of Bret. He appeared immediately.

"Hi," I said. "The ring worked on Salome. I'm ready for prime time if Sauron shows up."

"Is the video unit set up," he asked?

"Yep, I answered, "I'm looking at it now. All I see is the empty dining room at the hideout."

"Yeah, me too."

"I'm going to go see Jason and see if he can teach me how to teleport. Call if Bart shows up."

"OK."

Esme took me to see Jason. He took me to a room they used for beginning teleport training. It was basically a long hall with a large scale on the floor to mark off feet from the start.

My first lesson was just to teleport to a mark on the floor I could see. Jason did his little tickle in my brain and said, "OK, now visualize yourself standing on the ten foot mark. Go."

I looked at the ten on the floor and visualized myself standing there, and there I was. Just as easy as that.

He called out increasing numbers and I teleported there as easy as thinking about it. When I was at the end he yelled, "face the far wall and teleport back to the start. I couldn't see the start, but I knew what it looked like, so I did my visualization and it worked. I was standing right beside him. I was thrilled. Baby steps yes, but I could teleport.

We worked on technique. I learned to go to places I knew and that worked fine. I learned to go to people I knew, without knowing where they were. I had trouble going to locations I had only the coordinates for. I was never good at math and this seemed to be related. Jason knew about my visions and had me call up one. I chose Magellan and saw him in a pasture. Jason had me teleport to Magellan's location and return. It worked. Next I practiced moving objects with me. He sat me in an old rowboat in a shed then did the tickle thing again. I moved that old rowboat with me to my backyard in Seattle, then to the hotel where I had found Melanie. Then I brought it home.

Just then Bret called. All he said was, "Bart's here. Get ready."

I teleported to Esme's office and sat in front of the monitor. I had my sleep spell ready to say, "Bart is a creep, fall fast asleep." I watched the monitor and saw flickers of movement, but gone before I could say anything. Dammit, the field of view was too small. It was like looking through a telescope at a tennis match. Then the video went blank.

Bret called just to say, "Bart's thunderbolt fried the camera."

I had to go there. I visualized myself standing in the door to the dining hall and I was there. The noise was deafening. and beams of light like ray gun blasts were flashing across the room. I saw Bret flying above the kitchen as a beam from Bart narrowly missed him as he turned abruptly. I couldn't see Bart yet. He was on the far side of the kitchen wall. I edged around the outside wall, staying low, using the tables for cover. I moved slowly, not wanting to attract attention. I couldn't see Bart he was behind something. I raised a vision of Bret and thought, "Bret, try to get Bart to move up and to his left so I can see him."

I saw Bret dart to Bart's right and go low. It worked, Bart flew into my field of view. I recited my rhyme, "Bart is a ..." and everything went black.

I woke up in Bret's bed. He and the Doc were looking at me. The Doctor said, close call. You'll have a headache for a while. I fixed the damage and suppressed most of the pain. Aspirin should take care of the rest. You'll be fine with a few days rest. Oh, and stay away from combat zones. Bret and his friends play rough." He left.

Bret said, "Thanks Doc. and walked him out. Lucifer was laying beside my head on the pillow. He nuzzled my ear and said "Ack." I reached up and rubbed his ears. I sensed he was relieved I was back.

Bret came back and I asked, "What happened?"

He said, I got Bart in position and he shot a bolt at me. It bounced off my shield and hit the wall above you. The wall started coming apart so I shielded you and Bart teleported out. One of the stones hit you on the head before I got my shield over you. I teleported you back to the medical facility and Doc fixed you. Best medicine in the world. No one else could have saved you."

I asked, "I was injured?"

He looked grim and said, "A concrete block hit you on the crown of your head. Your brain was swelling rapidly. Doc healed you and re-grew the bone. You've been out for two days and you won't even have a scar to brag about. You were very brave and almost paid with your life. If your shield had been up you wouldn't have been injured. We make everyone in the field go through combat training is to ensure they don't forget their shield. It has to become instinctive or its forgotten in the heat of battle."

He knelt beside the bed and kissed me. Then he said, "You gave me quite a scare, Suzy. You've become very special to me and I couldn't bear to lose you. I'm glad I was there to help. Promise me you won't go into a battlefield again until you've been trained."

I was never more sincere than when I said, "I promise. You guys play too rough." Something was happening. The rings in my breasts were stirring. They were pulling me up.

I sat up to relieve the strain and Bret said, "You should lay down, Suzy."

I said, "I'm not doing it. the Rings are making me sit up. They're moving by themselves." I looked down at my chest. The rings were standing straight out from my chest and tenting the fabric. Bret backed up and the pull increased. I said, "Bret, they're pulling me to you. Don't move."

He leaned closer and the rings touched him. They gave me an instant orgasm and I grabbed Bret and pulled myself to him. The rings were holding me there anyway. but this felt better. He held me to him until the orgasm subsided. The rings were inert again.

"I have to go help look for Bart and the warheads. Esme will stay with you." He tried to kiss me on the forehead , but I grabbed him and turned it into a much more passionate experience. He sank to his knees and we kissed for a while. We broke and looked at each other. He got a huge grin on his face, said, " A treat to remember me by." His hand slid up under my nightgown and took hold of my left nipple ring.

Oh shit. My arousal was instantaneous. My belly surged into a second huge orgasm. I gasped and screamed in pleasure. I arched my back and grabbed hold of Bret. He was still grinning at me. The wonderful bastard. I loved him so. I poulled myself into him and he kept hold of my nipple ring. I had a third orgasm before I had come down from the first. I screamed again. He released my ring and I relaxed.

My belly was still pulsing and I had pumped my love juices onto his bed. I was laying in a spreading wet spot. It wasn't fair. I wasn't able to give him pleasure and I couldn't. I wanted him to touch me again. I said, "Bret, love, that's not fair. You can give me an orgasm with a single touch of your finger. I want to pleasure you too."

HE said, "Sorry love. I'm late and can't stay. Tonight though, we'll have more time."

I said, "Bret Thorne, you've become special to me also. Good luck and come back safe. Now go get him."

Chapter 19

Esme came in and handed me a yogurt and an apple. She had the same. We ate while we talked. She sat in a chair where I could see her. She said, "Hi. Welcome back. I assume Bret read you the riot act about always having your shield on?"

I said, "Yeah. Stupid, huh."

"Not per se," she said, "Bret's always going somewhere that's not safe. He has his up all the time and he just assumes the rest of us do too. If you're going to be around him then you should raise it whenever you get out of bed. Do you intend to be around him?"

OK. I should have expected this question. She is his sister. I carefully said, "Esme, I like your brother a lot. We've slept together several times and he is the best lover I've ever had. He knows how to treat a girl and his powers let him do things, go places, no mere mortal ever could. We're still learning each other. I could fall in love with him easily. But, and its a big but, I don't think he's ready to settle down. He's having too much fun saving the world. I want to learn what I can do and what he can do before we make any sort of commitment. I do so want to make him happy. I won't do anything to cause him hurt."

Esme said, " Thanks for that. I agree with you. Don't push him away. Just be his good friend for now. He's never had any close friends. His job always got in the way. But he could use one. There's no better way to learn about a man than to sleep with him. He's complex so I think you can learn something new about him for years."

"OK," I said, "new topic, were you able to find out if there is someone in MG who uses visions that I can talk to?"

She grimaced and said, "I asked Marcus and he looked. But he didn't find any record of anyone who used visions, or even had them. You're on your own with your visions. I'd be willing to help you experiment if you want. Besides that you can go see Dr. Garey. He knows more about how a wizard's brain works than anyone else. He's one himself and has approached our powers from an analytical view."

I didn't especially want someone poking around inside my head. It looked like my best option to learn more about how I worked. "I'm game. I guess seeing him would count as taking it easy. Would you contact him and get me in to see him. I'll get dressed."

Esme went in the living room and I looked through Bret's collection of girl's clothes in the closet. I chose a blouse and skirt. I looked around the bedroom and saw a dresser. One of the drawers had a label, "Suzanne." I opened it and saw some unmentionables and a jewelry box. I peeked inside and saw the clit ornament and the risqué necklace. They looked lonely and I guess they might be overdoing it with my new nipple rings. I closed the box and looked through the drawer. I found three black lace push-up bras. Three different sizes and the one that fit me was the smallest. We really needed to talk.

I went to the kitchen and found Esme sipping a cup of coffee. I was surprised to find one of those single cup at a time brewers like I had at home. I looked in the cupboards and found coffee. And, joy of joys, a plastic refillable coffee holder just like mine. Bret had investigated what I used and had borrowed, stolen, copied, or bought one for me. I crammed the holder full of ground coffee and soon was sipping a cup of my favorite rocket fuel. It was excellent coffee, too. Now I felt right at home. I sighed in pure bliss as I sipped.

I saw Esme watching me. She said, "Bret said you had specific tastes in coffee. I see you get an unusual amount of pleasure from it."

I smiled back and said, "Esme, I haven't had a good cup of coffee since I was in Seattle. It seems like a lifetime, so much has happened."

She said, "Four days, I think."

"Well, a lot's happened."

"Yes," she said, "its been a busy time. Are you ready to go see Dr. Garey?"

"So soon? I always have to schedule Dr's appointments a month in advance."

"Dr. Garey heard about your adventures and wanted to talk to you anyway. And he's not a medical Doctor. He's a scientist and not in so much demand. When you're ready I'll transport us. He's a ways away."

I finished my coffee and put the cup down and stood up. I said, "Let's go." This looked more like a psychiatrist's office not a lab. There was a man in a white lab coat sitting at a desk. Esme said, "Suzanne Ryder, meet Dr. Norman Garey. Norm, this is Suzy."

He stood up and shook my hand and said, "Pleased to meet you Ms. Ryder. How can I help you?"

Where to start? I said, "Doctor, I have visions. I want to keep them. They are quite useful in my business. I want to learn how to control them and make them more useful."

"He asked, "How are they useful?"

"I'm a private investigator. Many of my jobs requires me to locate a person or thing. If I have something of the person, a picture or something they've touched. Then I can close my eyes and see a vision of the person. Its like I'm looking at them and I can see things beyond them. Same thing with animals or objects. What I'd like is the ability to tell their location directly. "

He said, "I begin to understand. All of us that teleport have the ability to jump to a place they can visualize or to a set of coordinates they know. You'd like to be

186

able to revere that and get the coordinates of a place you can see in your vision. Right?"

"Yes, Doctor. Exactly right."

He stared past me and said, "Ms. Ryder, what you do with a vision is similar to what a teleport does. When she goes to a place where a person they know is at. Its not exactly the same, but the same area of your brain is definitely involved. I'd like to run some tests and see what I can learn. The tests are not invasive. I would ask you to wear a helmet and have you exercise your visions while I map the active areas ff your brain. We can do them in a half hour or so."

"OK," I said, "Let's do them."

He stood up and said my lab is next door. He opened the door and we followed him through it.

It was a big room and in its center was a bed with a cover over one end.

He walked to the bed and said, "This is a functional magnetic resonance imaging scanner. It doesn't use any invasive energy or devices. Its quite safe. You just lay in here and I'll talk to you through a speaker and ask you to do some mental exercises. The machine will see what's happening in different areas of your brain. I'll get

some pictures of your brain at work. When we're done I'll review them with you and see what conclusions we can draw. OK?"

It seemed simple enough, so I said, "OK, what do I do?"

"Take off your earrings and any other jewelry or metal in your clothing , please."

Oops. This should not be embarrassing. I didn't do it. Its not my fault. I said, "Doctor, due to an enchanted ring and our efforts to improve it. I now have two large, Gold rings in my breasts that I can't remove. Will they be a problem?"

His eyes got big. He looked at Esmerelda. She said, "Not her idea, Doc. It was an accident. I was there."

He opened his mouth, closed it, and said, "It won't hurt you, it might mess up the imaging. Let's see."

I handed my earrings to Esme and she grinned at me.

He said, now lay on your back on the bed. I lay down and he put a pillow under my head. Now don't move, please. The bed slid under the cover. It was a good thing I wasn't claustrophobic.

He gave me a series of simple instructions. Count to ten, open and close my eyes, mouth, move my fingers, etc. Then he said, "Try to have a vision of a person."

I closed my eyes and tried to get Bret. He popped up immediately and He said, Hi, Suzy. What's up. For the first time I just thought what I wanted to say. I didn't speak. I thought, Hi, Bret. I'm with Esme at Dr. Garey.

He trying to help me understand how I can improve my visions. I'm laying in one of his machines."

He replied, "Good idea. Nice talking to you. Good work on your telepathy, too. See you soon. Bye." And he winked out.

Dr. Garey asked, "Suzanne, did you have a talk with the person in your vision?"

"Yes, Doc."

"Good. Now you've started learning to fly, right?"

"Yes, a little."

"OK," he said, "try to lift just enough to be weightless without moving."

"Doc, I don't have good control yet, but I'll try."

I thought about lifting a little, then a little more, then I bumped against the cover. Damn. I lowered back onto the bed. I said, "Sorry, Doc."

He said, "That's OK. I got what I wanted and you didn't break anything. Now try to get a vision of an object. Tell me when you get it."

I tried for a vision of Bret's toothbrush. It popped up instantly. I said, "Got it."

Dr. Garey said, "Now try to read its location in relative coordinates. That is how far away and in what direction. Imagine your body is lying on the north-south line."

I looked at the image. I Visualized myself lying in the machine. I could see a line between my body and the toothbrush. I said, "Doc, it works. It is twelve thousand three hundred and fifty feet away and its almost due east of me."

I heard him say, "That's great, Suzy. I'm done for now. I'll come get you out of there."

He slid the bed out of the machine and said, "Come to the desk and I'll show you what your brain is doing.

He called up an image of what he said was my brain in action. He played the recording of our conversation while the image of the brain changed as if by magic. I watched my brain image change while I did the muscle control things. When I did something an area would change color from gray or black to an orange or yellow, sometimes red. He pointed out my vision area and muscle control and computations as they lit up. It was always one area that changed color.

He stopped the playback and said, "Suzy, up to now your brain behaved just like any healthy woman on the street. Perfectly normal and just like the medical students see in their training. Next we will see what it looks like when you call up a vision of Bret and talk with him. He started the playback and I heard his recorded voice tell me to get a vision of a person.

My brain image exploded in color five distinct areas were bright red. Dr. Carey pointed to them and said, "Vision, speech, memory, facial recognition, and reasoning. Suzy, these are what I see for teleportation plus facial recognition. You are effectively using sixty percent of your brain for this vision." He stopped the playback after the colors faded out. He continued, "This is one of the highest brain functions I've seen. I'm not surprised you haven't found another vision adept. This is an extraordinarily high brain function. Are you tired after a vision?"

I thought back, and said, "Not usually. If I keep one going for a long time I get hungry."

"OK," he said, "next I asked you to try and lift yourself. Here's what that looked like."

He started the playback and I watched my the colors start again. This time only three areas activated. He pointed to them and said, " Vision, Reasoning, and memory. This is a familiar pattern I've seen on other witches and wizards during flight. I can't tell what each area really does. But it seems reasonable that the reasoning center is responsible for the actual flight. Vision is likely your primary means of orientation. The memory function may have something to do with flight control, but that's just a guess. I'd like to have a blind, flight capable person to try this on, but none have shown up."

"But, Doctor, " I asked, "what does all this mean?"

He said, "It looks like your flight is normal. It also looks like your visions are using some of the same regions of your brain as teleportation.. Let me show you the last experiment results. They seem significant." He started the playback.

I watched the image start gray and black and this time three areas lit up. The doctor pointed to them and named them, "Vision, facial recognition, and reasoning. Keep watching, there's a change when you look for a vector."

I saw it change, another area lit up and the one he called reasoning doubled in brightness.. When it all went gray and black again he stopped the playback.

He said, "Here's how I interpret what's happening. Your vision of a person needs the facial recognition area. That may be a misnomer because you also used it when visualizing an object. Anyway, Your visions use the same functional areas of the brain as teleportation. I expect that you can do only one of those functions at a time. If you want to go to an object of your vision, first get the vision. Get its location from the vision, then turn off the vision and teleport. You should be able to teleport just fine with training. You should establish some clear distinctions between visions and teleporting. Maybe close your eyes only for visions and always teleport with them open. Just a suggestion. All right, I'm done for now and I have another job waiting. Goodbye."

We said our goodbyes and Esme took us to the cafeteria for lunch. Good solid healthy food like in a hospital cafeteria. I got a tray and plate. I reached for some lasagna and my rings shocked me. I snapped my hand back in surprise. My rings now were controlling my diet? I reached for some broccoli and nothing happened. I got some salad without incident. Blue cheese and ranch dressings got me shocked.. They let me have oil and vinegar. I was zapped when I tried to get a piece of cake. Shit.

While we ate I asked, "Esme, do you think I could get Jason to give me some more teleportation training? I think it might help me look for the nukes."

She said, "Sure. It looks like a teleport's location skills might improve your vision's location skills too. There's no higher priority right now than finding those babies." She took us to Jason and we explained what I needed.

He said, "OK. That's Teleporting 105: 'Where am I.' I'll give you that in about an hour of class work and an hour of practical experience. We went to a classroom and he brought a map up on a big display in the front of the room.

He showed me coordinate systems and how they worked. Every now and then I would feel that unique little tingle in my brain as he adjusted something. It was uncanny.. It was effective. If this sort of education was available, student would learn everything for a degree in a month. When class was over I had a detailed 3D image of he world in my head. I knew every major city, every political boundary. Detailed topography and I instinctively knew the date and time where I was.

He said, time for some practical training. I will give you a location and you will teleport yourself and me there. OK?

I said, "OK."

He said, "Shield up, invisibility on, center of Caracas, Venezuela."

I concentrated and it worked, sort of. I had dropped us in traffic at the intersection of Av. Nueva Granada and Av. Roosevelt with traffic whipping by us. Oops. I quickly moved us a couple of blocks to the grounds of Escuela Gran Colombia.

Jason said, calmly, "When I go somewhere unfamiliar, I hover ten or twenty feet off the ground. At least until I see what's happening there."

I said, "You could have told me that earlier."

He smiled and said, "You'll remember it much better now."

He bounced us all over the planet. He would take us places and ask where we were, or he would give me a location by coordinates, or a name. We visited every continent. I saw deserts, fighting in Afghanistan, cities, Mount Everest. Finally he said, "Back to MG." I looked at him blankly. I don't know where it is."

He said, "Think back. Where did we start from."

I recalled our start in a classroom and its coordinates popped into my mind. I took us there. I was careful to stay low, under the ceiling.

Jason said, "Your mind will remember any place you've been and you can return there."

I asked, "Does that include places I was at before I met you?"

He smiled, "No, not unless you've been there a lot, like your house. You're done for today. Go see Esme."

Chapter 20

I pictured Esmerelda and knew where she was. I could see her in her office. I popped in and sat in her guest chair. Lucifer jumped into my lap. I looked at him with a new respect. He could teleport and had known how without my training. And he could find me too. I said, "Nice to see you, Lucifer. Hi Esme. I think I'm close to being ready to try and find those nukes."

Esmerelda says, "What do you want to do now?"

"I'm new to this magic stuff. Is there a way to try and hide things by magic?

"Sure. first, you've only been exposed to what you can do with your body, right?"

"Yeah? There's more?"

"Esme said, cryptically, "Spells."

"Spells," I said. "How do they work, exactly?"

She said, "A wizard or witch can cast a spell on a thing or a person. You've heard the Shakespeare passage from The Tempest,

> *'Fillet of a fenny snake,*
>
> *In the cauldron boil and bake;*
>
> *Eye of newt and toe of frog,*
>
> *Wool of bat and tongue of dog,*
>
> *Adder's fork and* blind-worm's *sting,*
>
> *Lizard's leg and howlet's wing,*

For a charm of powerful trouble,
Like a hell-broth boil and bubble."'

"Yes," I said, "its vaguely familiar."

"Well, its not like that at all. A witch casts a spell by envisioning what they want to happen. Then lays it on the subject like winding a piece of yarn around it. You need to develop a 'second sight' to see the spell. When you do, it looks like a mass of different colored spaghetti or yarn wound around and around. If you're as strong as the person who cast the spell, you can break it by unwinding the yarn."

"How," I asked, "do I develop my second sight?"

She said, "I can help with that." She picked up a pen from her desk. Watch." I looked at the pen and it disappeared. Slowly, from one end to the other it faded out in about a second.

"I take it you put a spell of invisibility on the pen?"

She said, "Right. Now look where my hand is. I'm holding it. Focus on my hand. Now unfocus. Imagine you are looking across infinite space. Let your mind disbelieve everything you see."

I struggled with the concept and I felt that familiar tickle in my head. Then I could see the ball of vibrantly colored spaghetti in her hand. I couldn't see the pen, but I could see the ends of a strand. I reached out to it with ghostly fingers and unwrapped the pen. The strands fell apart and disappeared as I unwound them. When they were all gone, I blinked and everything was normal and I could see the pen in her hand.

"Spooky," was all I could say.

"Now," she said, "you have your second sight. You have a lot of power in you, Suzanne." You can cast a spell on almost anything to do almost anything. Only a more powerful wizard or witch can undo it. Also, most spells fade overt time. When I looked at your ring and then your nipple rings I could see the enchantment. I think it was enchanted by Asmodeus or some other God or Demon, because it is very strong magic. Bret is the strongest wizard I know and he couldn't touch it. Now they've been enhanced even more by our efforts. Use your second sight to look at your rings."

I unbuttoned my blouse and pulled my bra down. I did the unfocus trick and saw the enchantment. It looked like a glowing, translucent strand of pink wrapped around the ring many times. I didn't see an end. I pulled the bra back up and buttoned my blouse. "I saw it," I said, "and it looked strong. So, does this mean a wizard could wrap an invisibility spell around the nukes and I couldn't see them?"

"No," she said, "with an invisibility spell around the nukes, you couldn't see them. A talented person, using second sight, could see the spell. So you need to be able to use your vision and switch in and out of second sight while looking. That may take some practice."

"Its going to be harder than I first thought," I said. "I'm going to have to practice locating my vision and switching in and out of second sight at the same time. Anything else?"

"Well," she said, "a competent wizard will lay false trails and layer his spells. So they have to be unwrapped one at a time."

"Just frigging gets better all the time."

"On the bright side," she said, "he likely does not know about your vision ability. That's new and so he won't protect against it."

I thought about the problem. I said, "My visions won't do any good if he can make the nukes invisible to my vision. Its not the same as normal seeing. We need to test that. I'd like to get Bret or someone else as strong as Bart to make some strong spells."

Esme said, "Call Bret. It shouldn't take but a few minutes for him to set up some test objects."

So I called him and he came instantly. As soon as he appeared my rings pulled me to him. My arousal shot through the roof. I asked "Esme, would you step outside for a moment, my rings are making me orgasm?"

She surprised me by coming around her desk. She pulled out my blouse and reached her fingers in to touch one of my rings. Both of our bodies spasmed into instant orgasms and we screamed our pleasure.

Bret grabbed me as Esme lay against her desk, scrunched into an orgasm. Bret and I kissed until the orgasm subsided. My rings quieted and Esme and I resumed out positions, a little embarrassed and wet between our legs.

Esme said, "Sorry, but when that train leaves the station, I'd like to ride too."

I replied, "Might as well. I'm not in control and the company's fine."

Bret had watched our orgasms with amusement. He listened to our request. He said, OK. I'll make ten things and I'll give you pictures of some, pictures and a part of some and let you touch some. OK?

I said, "That ought to do it."

He vanished and was back in fifteen minutes carrying a box. In the box was a ruler, a pen, a pencil, a picture of an eraser, a picture of a cup, a picture of a teapot and the top to the teapot, a picture of a spoon and fork, a fork, a picture of a candle, a half of a candle, a picture of a dog, a dog collar, a C-size battery and a picture of a flashlight. He also had a sheet of paper with all the things listed.

He said, "Look at all this stuff and don't touch anything yet. When you're ready, I'll take the ruler, pen and pencil away. I'll put an invisibility spell on all the things and send them far away. I'm sure size doesn't matter. Distance might, the spells might matter and whether they're in motion might. So I'll put some in stationary and mobile places all over the globe. I'll come back and we'll go together to look for them. I'm your guard on this outing."

I said, "Go to it Bret. Hurry back."

Esme and I looked at each other. I said, I wish I'd gotten a cup of coffee before now. I could use it."

She said. Go to Bret's place and make it. I'll tell him where you've gone if he comes here. He' likely just to come to you anyway. Wizard, you know?"

"Right. Bye." and I transported out to Bret's place.

I started my Rocket Fuel flowing in the Keurig maker and watched it dribble out. I felt Bret's arm go around me in a snug embrace. I could tell it was him from his aroma. I don't know how to describe it, but I'd know his scent anywhere. He slid a hand up my chest and fondled my breast in passing. Then he reversed direction and slid it down inside my blouse and into my bra. At the last instant I knew what he was doing and I welcomed it. His questing finger touched my nipple ring and my loins burst into a huge orgasm. My love juices drenched my panties and I screamed in pleasure. He was holding me up so I couldn't collapse to the floor. My legs lifted off the ground as I curled into a fetal position hanging from his mighty arms. My pussy spasmed over and over trying to grasp the missing penis. It was wonderful, but I wanted him in me so bad. When my body was under control again, I said, "Put me down you big lunk."

When my feet hit the floor I spun around and leapt into his arms and kissed him hard and long. When I broke apart I said, "Thank you so much Darling, but it would be so much better if we did this the old fashioned way. I want you in me."

He said, "I thought you were in a hurry, Suzy."

I replied, "I want to be asked before I have an orgasm, OK?"

He smiled and said, "But I like giving you presents, Love. Are you ready to start the treasure hunt?"

I was sure I wasn't going to win the orgasm argument, so I said, "Right. Let's go. How do I start?"

He said, "I put ten enchanted objects somewhere on the Earth. Big place. Why don't you start at the top of the list and work down? Oh. and for incentive, whenever you find one, you get an orgasm. OK?"

I said, "OK. Its a fine incentive. Now I'm looking for a ruler." I remembered touching it. I closed my eyes and tried for a vision. Nothing. I remembered to try for a second sight. It was hard to combine with a vision. I forced my mind's eye to look into infinity and I saw the ruler. It was wrapped in the glowing spaghetti. I couldn't see an end to unwrap, but I got a location. It was in Bret's shower. I opened my eyes and said. That was too easy. Its in your shower."

My blouse and bra vanished. My rings stood up and pulled me to Bret. He reached out one finger and touched my right ring. He was ready and grabbed me as I spasmed into a strong orgasm. He held me up and I felt my undies and skirt vanish. I felt something else and when I was able I looked down and found I was wearing an adult diaper. I said, "Good thinking. I'm going to find every one of your objects now."

Bret said, "I wanted to give you confidence to start. The rest aren't quite so close. Find the pen."

I thought back to the pen and what it looked like. I remembered its feel and closed my eyes. I called up a vision and got one, but it wasn't one. It was like one of those bug eye view kaleidoscopes. There were dozens of them, all just alike. I tried my second sight. No dice. Nothing there. I went back to normal vision and tried for a location and got dozens of locations, hundreds of miles apart. My eyes still closed, I sad, "Bret. You cheated. There are dozens of the pens."

He said, Bart may make duplicates, too. Look closely. I zoomed in on one pen. Nothing. I switched, at the speed of thought, looking for something unique. I looked closer and closer, finally, I saw a difference. I yelled, "I found it. You bastard."

I opened my eyes and he said, "What did you find?"

"My fingerprint you sneaky bastard."

"Congratulations, that was a hard one and you found it. I made sixty duplicates before I gave that one to you. Bart may do the same thing, so you know what to do now. But there's more to this one. How many pens did you see?"

"I didn't count them."

"Go back and count them."

"OK." I started my vision again and counted thirty five. I said, "Thirty five."

He said, OK. This was also a distance test. I put them four hundred miles apart, evenly spaced. Floating at two hundred feet above the ground around the equator. Since you see thirty five, your visions reach about seven thousand miles from you. Good coverage, but we may have to move around a bit to find the nukes. Try the pencil now."

"OK, but I'm still going to call you 'sneaky bastard' from now on."

He smirked and said, "Higher praise I could not desire. ready for your reward?" He beckoned me with a finger. I responded by bounding to him. He touched my left ring this time with an identical result. When I could stand he released me. I stood a little shaky for a moment.

He asked, "The pencil?"

I said, "OK." I called up my vision and didn't see anything so I tried my second sight and got it . But as I looked at it, it faded out. What did he do now? I turned off my second sight and found it. I tried to get a location, but if t faded out again. He had somehow made his spell oscillate on and off. It didn't stay in one state long enough for me to get a location. I tried teleporting it back to me but that didn't work in either state. He must have protected it somehow. When I could see it in normal sight I teleported a paper clip right next to it, figuring I could find the paper clip. I changed my vision to the paper clip and found it. I got a location and watched the location changing rapidly. Thousands of miles an hour. What the fuck did he do? I opened my eyes and looked at Bret's grinning face. He knew he had been clever and was proud of himself. I said, "How did you do that?"

He said, "I wrapped an oscillating invisibility spell around the pencil. I stuck it to the shell of a GPS satellite in low earth orbit with some space qualified glue from the Soviets. I'll take it off and bring it back to Earth. Remember, Bart could do something like this with his Nukes. Hard to find if its in Space and we only look on Earth. The paper clip was a good idea and would have worked in most locations."

Damn. He was right. I needed to look outside the box. I smiled at him and said , "Thanks. You cheated. Do I get my reward for this one?" I said this in a light-hearted tone, but I felt a desperate need for the orgasm. my belly was clenching and I felt a hunger greater than I should. I wanted to orgasm so bad it was a physical pain in my loins.

He said, "You found it and I cheated, so yes."

My rings drug me to him, faster than I could walk. I was literally yanked to him. I didn't care. I wanted that orgasm. Now.

He reached out his finger and touched my ring. I orgasmed as quick, as strong as before. He held me up or I would have collapsed. It was so strong. I felt limp, weak, and so good. My belly spasmed repeatedly. I felt my juices flowing through my pussy and flooding the diaper. I needed to be changed soon. I felt the liquid weighting it down. I didn't know where Bret got it.

"Bret," I said, "I'm filling this diaper. Could I have another, plcase?"

He smirked and said, "Want to be changed, baby?"

I smiled and said, "Unless you want me to overflow. Yes, please."

I felt the exchange and I was dry again. I said, "Thank you."

We continued the search. We had to travel since several were out of range. Bret took my diaper away and I didn't get another one. Unnecessary since my orgasms just resulted in my fertilizing the plants. I stayed invisible with my shield up so clothes were unnecessary. I felt quite risqué traveling the world naked.

I found the eraser in a town in Maine and the teacup in Palm Springs. The cup was in the dining car of the California Zephyr. I couldn't get a vision of any of the others from MG so we traveled. I found the candle half in Australia deep in a mine. The dog was in the hold of a SAS 380 en route to Amsterdam and I put his collar back on him. The spoon was in a coffee house in Brussels being used by a customer. The flashlight was in the pack of a Sherpa leading a party up K-2.

Bret gave me an orgasm every time I found one. My body was now demanding another one as soon as I started looking for the next missing object. My rings were helping. As soon as I earned an orgasm they yanked me toward Bret. If he dawdled or teased me they would shock me in impatience. I hurt too much to wait. I found myself pleading with him to hurry up. I asked him to give me extra orgasms during the long searches. I didn't realize it but I was becoming conditioned to beg him for orgasms. He was becoming even more powerful.

We couldn't think of anything else Bart might have done to hide the nukes so we were ready to go. Tomorrow. We went back to Bret's apartment and didn't get much sleep. We made love several times and he touched my rings a couple of other times. He liked to watch me orgasm and I loved it too.

My rings made me follow him around. If he was in another room my rings would tingle and eventually start shocking me until I went into the room he was in. I didn't have to touch him, but the rings wanted me to be with him. The rings wouldn't let me get dressed when we got home. I tried a couple of times, but the rings shocked me whenever I touched my clothing.

In the morning it was worse. My rings wouldn't let me get far enough away from him to get dressed or eat, or anything. I trailed him around the apartment like his slave girl. Naked and being led around by the big gold rings in my nipples. He asked me what I was doing and I explained I had no choice. He offered to help by going to the places I needed to be to get dressed or anything else. It didn't help. If I tried to get dressed the rings shocked me. I was to stay naked. The rings closely monitored my food choices. I was allowed to eat yogurt and all bran with skim milk. Brct helped me by materializing different foods until he got something I was allowed to eat.

After eating I became aroused. The rings wanted me to have another orgasm. Bret, "I said, "my rings are making me aroused. Would you take me now?"

He smiled and said, "My pleasure Suzy. What will you do when I'm away?"

I replied, I guess I'll have to ask Esme or someone else to give me an orgasm."

He said, "Would you like me to replace that chastity belt?"

I said, "No way. Just come here, my love."

He took me in the bedroom and then he took me on the bed. It was heavenly. Much better than doing it alone.

Chapter 21

He said he had a few things to coordinate and then we'd start on the snipe hunt. He disappeared. As soon as he was gone my rings settled down. I went into the closet and looked in the mirror. My body had continued to match itself to a perfect girl's shape. I measured myself. 38-24-36. My breasts were conical and erect. They looked like a teenager's, except for the rings, of course. My nipples had grown too. They were over an inch long and a half inch in diameter. The rings let me get dressed. They made me wear a skirt and wouldn't allow any undies. They wanted me ready for action, I guess.

I teleported to Esme and told her about the searches and all the dirty tricks Bret had played with them. I also told her about the control the rings had exerted over me. I wanted her to know what was happening if they started again. We talked about the ring's independent actions. Esme opined it was likely due to the enhanced power we had given the ring. It might subside once we had used the ring on Bart. I hoped so. I was tired of having a pair of sex starved gold rings leading me around by my nipples. I noticed I was becoming needy again. Less than an hour and my body was nudging me. Letting me know by the twitching and itching in my loins that I hadn't come in too long a time. I was being conditioned to need to release many times a day. I was becoming addicted to orgasms, if not love.

Bret stepped into the room and my rings went crazy. They yanked me into his arms and gave me a big damned orgasm. If he hadn't caught me I would have been rolling around on the floor moaning. As it was I writhed in his arms, moaning. I saw the joy in his eyes. He held such power that his mere presence could drive me into an orgasm. Make me helpless in his arms. It was so true. Not all my fault, but truth, anyway.

I was embarrassed by my helpless need. I somehow felt I was letting down women everywhere. I should be strong and rational. Dole out my favors to maximize my power and benefit. Ration my body so that men need me. But I was helpless to control my needs. They were overwhelmingly powerful. They swamped rational thought and defeated all my feminist training. I was not powerful and I feared I would never have any power over my needs again. I was a slut, a sex slave, addicted to my man. I would do whatever he wanted just so he would give me another orgasm. I had been ringed by the power of Asmodeus, the demon of lust, and cursed with terrible need.

He set me back on my feet and I said, "I need to visit the ladies room and then I'll be ready to go."

Bret said, "I've got everything ready for you in the gym. We'll go there when you're ready."

I cleaned up my love juices and went back to Esme's office. Bret transported us down to the gym. Bart had taken ten W76 nuclear warheads intended for Trident missiles. Bret had assembled pictures of the actual warheads and their internals in the gym. He also had packing materials and the storage cradles they had rested in lined up on the gym floor. I went to the first one, and studied the materials. I felt the packing cases and the cradles. Bret had a chair and a desk for me. I sat down and Lucifer jumped in my lap.

I looked at the photo and tried for a vision. Nothing. I changed to second sight. Again nothing. I said, "I get nothing. its probably out of range. Lets take a trip."

Bret got Sam and Mack in the gym and we mapped out a set of stops. The first pass would move around the equator in six thousand mile hops. We'd start at St. John's, Newfoundland. Then Casablanca, Morocco, then Baku, Azerbaijan, and finally, Seattle, United States.

Before we set off Bret gave us some briefing papers from the US government. Sauron had set up an online auction for the ten warheads. Every terrorist organization and rogue country was raising hard currency to bid. The auction had started already. North Korea had won the bidding for the first weapon. The CIA believed the North Koreans wanted to reverse engineer the warhead. They already had developed long range ballistic missiles. They had yet to build weapons small and light enough for the missiles to carry them to the US.

Bret transported us to St. John's, Newfoundland, and into a room in the Murray Premises Hotel. He told me the MG has a permanent room in every city in the world. I sat in an easy chair in the main room of the suite and Lucifer jumped in my lap. I Spread out the pictures of the warheads on the floor and closed my eyes. Nothing. Second Sight. Nothing. I said, "Getting nothing her either." We gathered up our stuff and Bret took us onward.

Our next stop was Casablanca, Morocco. The MG had a lot of pull or money or both. He took us to a penthouse suite on the Riad Jnane Sherazade. A 5-star hotel in downtown Casablanca. I wish we had more time to spend in these fine places. Not now, but I'd make Bret take me to every one of them. Bret heard me whine and said He'd bring me back to these places and more. We set up again and I got nothing again. Next stop, Baku, Azerbaijan.

In Baku we teleported into another penthouse suite on top of the Excelsior Hotel and Spa. Another 5-star hotel, but considerably different. We were getting speedy at getting me set up. Soon I was in a chair with Lucifer in my lap and photos spread out before me. I closed my eyes and got nothing. I switched to second sight and I saw something. It was hazy and indistinct. Not good enough to work from. I opened my eyes and said, "I got something on second sight but it was at my limit and I couldn't get anything like a location from it. Let's move on. First, I need to talk to Bret in private."

He looked at me and smiled. He led me into the master bedroom and said, "I've stayed here before. Its a very nice hotel and they take great care in protecting their visitors sleep. The bedrooms are soundproofed."

I said, "That's good news, because we're going to test it. I need you right now. I've been holding it in for two continents." I stripped off my skirt and I was ready. His clothes dropped onto the floor behind him and I jumped into his arms. He was careful not to let my rings touch him yet. He laid me on the bed and I spread my legs as far apart as I could and put my arms behind my head. I closed my eyes and said, I'm so ready. Take me, sir, please. I felt him lower himself onto me and his wonderfully big, stiff cock slid silently into my sopping wet pussy. I let out a gasp of shock and pleasure as he tripped every nerve in my body with his rampant invasion. He pumped me up two or three times and I was ready to blow. As he slid in the third time he closed his hand around one of my nipple rings and I exploded into a huge orgasm. My love juices flooded into my pussy and my belly spasmed ferociously. I felt my muscles clamp down on his huge cock as he slid in and out. I clamped my mouth around his pectoral muscle and tried to stifle my screams of pleasure.

He kept his hand clamped on my nipple ring and as soon as my orgasm wound down another one hit me. It was bigger than the first. I kept my hands behind my head with fierce pride. I wouldn't move them. I knew he liked them there. My belly pulsed in furious spasms, over and over. I felt him explode into me, filling me with his hot spend and I orgasmed yet again. It was too much. I fainted dead away. I woke up alone in the bed in the middle of a large wet spot. I got up and found Bret in the bathroom washing blood off his chest. He turned to me and said, "I guess you didn't believe me about the sound proofing, huh?"

I said , "I'm so sorry. It was a reflex. It was the only way I knew to keep quiet. Are you All right.?"

He pointed to a pink spot on his chest. "Already healed," he said. "One of the perks of my profession."

We got dressed and went back to the others. They had the stuff packed up and were ready to go. They didn't say anything but I'm sure they knew what we were doing.

Bret took us to Seattle, to my house. I set up in the dining room and Lucifer jumped into my lap. I closed my eyes and got nothing then switched to second sight. I saw them. Ten coils of spell spaghetti. Close together, but not in the same building. I got a location in the Pacific. An Island. I didn't know what was there. I opened my eyes and gave the coordinates to Bret. He took us there. Invisible, shields up, floating a thousand feet over Caroline Island, Kiribati. Is was uninhabited save for one homestead. Now that we were at the island, I wasn't needed to find the warheads. They all saw the spells with their second sight. Now I was here just to zap Bart if we found him. Bret and I went to the homestead. It was the only house on the island and a likely place to find Bart. The house was built by Urima Felix, a French Polynesian entrepreneur. With the agreement of the Kiribati

Government. He kept us invisible. I took over my flight, invisibility, and shield as he dropped to the grounds below. I dropped down behind some coconut trees and looked for Bart. I had my sleep spell ready to use as soon as I laid eyes on him.

There was a tremendous crash and I saw Bart fly into the air with Bret right behind him. Bret hit Bart with a thunderbolt at close range and Bart tumbled out of the sky. Bret swooped down right behind him and slammed him into the ground. Bart stopped moving and looked stunned. Then he recovered and threw Bret into the air. Bret dove onto Bart again and pinned him down. I looked around the tree and got a clear view of Bart. I said me spell and it worked. Bart stopped moving and Bret waved me over. I flew into Bret's arms and we kissed. We landed and Bret asked, " Do you have your second spell ready?"

"Of course, I smirked."

I looked down at Bart, peacefully sleeping and said, "Bart has led a life of crime, now it is his time, to put aside this life of crime, and so when he feels a need, for a dastardly deed, he must take time to plant his seed, and will hurry home, to love Salome."

As soon as I said it, I felt a great relief, like a weight had left my shoulders. I had to test it. I said, Bret, quick, I think I've used up the extra energy. Would you touch one of my rings and see if I orgasm?"

I pulled out my top and he reached his fingers in and touched a ring. Nothing happened. Thank god I was

216

free of my orgasmic curse. Suddenly I felt arousal. Maybe there was a little left in the rings or maybe it was just Bret's normal affect on me. But I didn't orgasm. I pulled his hand out and said, "Later. Let's get the warheads and Bart home first."

He looked a little disappointed and said, "Guess you're cured. Good."

He sent Bart back to Esme who put him with Salome, still sleeping.

Bret, Sam, and Mack pulled the invisibility spells off the warheads. Verified the serial numbers and sent them back to Bangor. We all went back to HQ Bret sent the rest of the stuff back to the Navy.

I went to Bret's apartment and showered. Bret joined me in the shower in a few minutes. I was relieved to find his mere touch on one of my rings didn't trigger an immediate orgasm. It was nice though. Now they were just ornaments. I asked him, "Should I keep these rings? Do you like them?"

He said, "Let's see." He put his hands on my waist and turned me around. He looked at my rings and replied, I like them very much. I think you should keep them, but just for me, OK?"

I asked, "Do you think I or you, rather, could make them a little smaller? They're quite heavy."

He stared at them and said, "Use your second sight and look at them."

Oh no. Still enchanted? I looked at them with my second sight and they looked just like before. Wrapped in pink spaghetti spell strands.

Bret said, "It looks like the spell has to wear off before we can make any changes. I could try to break the spell, but if it was laid on by Asmodeus, it will need a demon or angel to lift it. Sorry."

Bummer. Well, at least I could cover them up. I wonder if they now act like the original ring? Will they shrink if I use them to make lovers unite? Worth a try I guess. We dried each other off and dressed. I looked at the women's clothes Bret had provided. They were all more revealing than I would have chosen for myself, but I was a new person now, thanks to the ring. I used to be a little ashamed of my tomboy build and covered it up more than I probably should have. Now I looked like I should be a model, so Bret's choice of female clothing was quite reasonable I decided. I was able to put on a thong and a push up bra without a murmur from my rings. I chose a short skirt and a translucent blouse with a short jacket. I looked in the mirror when I finished. I looked like Scarlett Johansen. Good enough. Today we had to go interview Bart and Salome, to see if he was still a threat.

I walked into the living room. Bret was talking on a telephone. I wasn't sure he used a phone. I was glad we didn't need them anymore. Maybe I should get his phone number though. I wasn't sure when I'd want to use the phone with him, but who knows? I looked at his face. He looked unhappy. He hung up and looked at me thoughtfully.

I asked, "What's up?"

He said, slowly, "That was the Navy. One of the warheads we sent back to them is empty. The physics package is missing. They'd really like it back. Their surmise is that North Korea only wanted the warhead to reverse engineer it. They left the casing as unnecessary. I need to go to Bangor and get the stuff back for that one. They'll be ready for me in a half hour. In the meantime, let's go see Bart and Salome. I'll call Esme and get her to meet us in detention."

Part 5 : All in a Days Work

Chapter 22

He teleported us to the detention level and he got the warden to put Bart and Salome in the interrogation room..

I was relieved to see Bart and Salome were dressed in casual clothes. No more black leather. Both of them looked a lot less menacing now.

On one side of the table Bart and Salome sat, holding hands and looking like lovers who had been caught toilet papering the neighbor's house. On the other side of the table was me, Esme, and Bret. We looked uncomfortable, like we had caught our friends in some petty theft. We did not look like we were happy we had caught a gang of international terrorists.

When you got down to what was important, Bart and Salome loved each other. Esme was the sister of both Bart and Bret. I loved Bret. I don't know if he loved me, but I was certain he was fond of me and we were at least friends with benefits.

Esme started the conversation, "Bart, do you know how many people died because of your actions?"

Bart said, surprisingly, "Of course. No one died because of me.

Bret said, "Bart, I saw the bodies of the men you sent to attack Bangor."

Bart smirked, "Brother, did you touch any of the fallen?"

Bret said, ""No. But the Marines were shooting at them and they were on the ground."

Bart replied, "I wanted a diversion so I could swipe the warheads. My 'Army' only had blanks. I wrapped a shield around them set to put them to sleep and dissolve when hit by a bullet. They're all back in prison now."

I piped up, "What about Ralph Henry. He was killed by your thugs or you."

He said, "No, he wasn't killed. He died of a massive stroke. We couldn't save him."

Bret asked, "What about the people who would die if the terrorists had gotten the warheads."

Bart smiled, and said, "I wasn't going to let them keep them. I just wanted their money. Besides, I was pretty sure you'd find them before I could sell them anyway. In fact all I got was the North Korean's money."

Bret asked, "How much did they pay you?"

Bart's smile grew larger and he replied, One billion dollars. They're going to be broke a long time, but it was a good deal for them. They'd spend twice that on research to develop a warhead like that. Anyway I planned to steal it back from them once they get it home. Theft is not hard when I'm invisible, bulletproof and can teleport through walls."

Bret said, "You almost killed Suzy when we were fighting in your hole in the ground."

Bart looked surprised and said, "That was just you and me. No one got hurt."

Bret replied, "Yeah. She did. You knocked down a wall and a concrete block hit her on the head. Her skull was cracked and only because I got her to our healer in time is she OK."

Bart was anguished. He looked at me and said, "Suzy, I'm so sorry. I didn't know you were there. Why didn't you have your shield on? Bret and I play rough, we always have. But we never fight where someone else can get hurt."

I felt sorry for him. It was my fault, at least partly. I had snuck into their battle ground to help Bret. I looked at Bret and asked, "was that a usual fight?"

He looked sheepish when he said, "Yeah. I'm afraid so. Bart and I are pretty evenly matched and fight each other to a standstill unless one of us makes a mistake. Hell, Suzy, I tried to keep you out of that cavern because I know how hard we fight. I didn't want you in there. I should have known how determined you are. I'm so sorry you got hurt."

I said, "No, you guys, it was my fault. I had no idea what such a battle could be like. I thought if I stayed far enough away I'd be safe. I was imagining you two like gladiators or boxers. I had no idea you would hurl lightning bolts at each other. Bret tried to keep me away and I never told him I was coming. Suddenly I was in War of the Worlds, or Clash of the Titans and All I could do was hide. I should have had my shield up. Don't either of you blame yourself for my injury. It was all my fault."

Esme said, "Guys, no one is safe when you fight. Hell, Bart, what you did gave the North Koreans enough to toss the world into a brawl. Except now millions of innocents get killed."

Bart said, "OK guys. I never intended for the Koreans to get their hands on one of the warheads. When they won the auction I showed their people the thing and promised to deliver it to the ship they had waiting. I never delivered it and I wasn't going to, either. You showed up on my island before I delivered it. Last I knew it was safe there.

I said, "Bret, do the North Koreans have any wizards or witches?"

Bret looked at Esme and Bart, then turned to me, and said, "Suzy, I don't know for sure. Talents seem to be almost randomly scattered among humans. I've found people with latent talent most places I've gone. As far as I know only the US and the old USSR ever had programs to actively look for people with psionic abilities. So, the North Koreans might have some."

I continued my thought, "We should find out and, if so, let the government know. This might change their thinking on magical defense."

Bret said, "Right. But first we need to find the physics package they got. Bart, we recovered all the warheads, but one was missing its guts. Suzy can find it, probably, and I'm going to get it back. Will you help us?"

Bart said, "OK, but you need to forget any charges against Salome or me. She'll help too and she's a potent witch."

Bret looked at Esme and she nodded agreement. He said, Bart, Salome, you're now part of the team. No more showboating though. Save that for after hours. About time, Bart."

Esme took Bart and Salome up to find them quarters. I said, "Bret, Bart and Salome are both magic users. Why didn't they just teleport out of detention?"

Bret smiled and said, "Suzy, I once drew an analogy between magic and 'The Force' from Star Wars. We built our HQ around a dead area. There's no 'Force' in a dead area., so magic doesn't work there. That's not quite right. Magic can't originate there. Magic can be done elsewhere and have an effect there. That's really why your ring didn't work down here the first time. It worked down here the next time because you were in Esme's office when you used it. See?"

I thought about it. I snarled, "Does that mean I didn't need to get my ring supercharged to affect Salome? Did I get these nipple rings for nothing?"

He smiled and said, "I'm sure you needed to get supercharged to affect Bart. He a strong wizard. The nipple rings are just our secret now. If it matters, you look sexy as hell with them and every time I see them I want to lick them clean. I'm glad you have them."

He came closer and we kissed. He was magical in so many ways. I just melted into him and he held me close. We hit so well together. My skin was tingling and my belly was heating up when Bart, Salome, and Esme appeared in the room behind Bret. Esme said, "Hey guys, I'm glad you like each other, but we have a planet to save. Come on."

Bret and I broke our kiss. He said, "Esme's our older sister and grew up ordering Bart and I around. She's never forgotten how."

Bret continued, OK. Plans. First thing is to go to Bangor and get the stuff for Suzy to find the missing pieces. She finds them, Bart and I take them . We all go back to Bangor with them. Then, we look for North Korean witches and wizards. Esme is our best telepath and can find talents and communicate with them, even if they only speak Korean. So we go back and Esme finds them. the government is holding their families hostage for their good behavior. If they want to leave, we get them out of there. OK?"

No one seemed to have any problems with the plan so we all nodded.

Bret said with emphasis, looking at me, "From now on everyone keeps their shields up tight. Even if we're in a 'safe' place. OK?"

We all nodded again and he took us to a warehouse where I saw many of the pictures of the warheads from before. The actual casing that was missing its guts was there. I handled everything and tried for a vision. Nothing. Second sight also nothing.

I turned to Bret and said, we need to get closer. He moved us to another penthouse on top of the Lotte Hotel in Seoul, South Korea. I laid out all the photos and Lucifer jumped in my lap. I closed my eyes and I got a vision in normal sight. I got a location and asked, "Do we have a map of North Korea?"

Bret unfolded a map on the dining table. I pointed to a spot. "Right here," I said.

Bret looked at it and said, "Bakcheon Nuclear Facility. Its mostly underground. OK folks, Suzy has found it. We're all going. Esme, you and Salome are looking for witches and wizards. If you find any transport them to HQ detention ASAP. If you need help, yell. Suzy, You need to focus on the exact location of the physics package. I'll read the location and transport us all there. Bart and I will take care of any guards, Bart, don't kill them unless its necessary. Just sending them to the surface a few miles away should be good enough. Everyone get your shields on maximum. And go invisible now. Anyone there will shoot us on sight. Get ready, we go on three."

It was exciting. I needed to pee, but I just turned on my shield and went invisible.

Bret said, "One..Two..Three."

I was standing in a large room with instruments and cabinets lining the walls. There was a couple of tables in the center of the room. Three oriental men were doing something with the stuff on the table. I recognized the physics package. There was a couple, a man and woman, standing off to the side, watching the men at the table. The woman looked alarmed and grabbed the man's arm. He looked surprised. They both vanished. I heard Esme in my mind. "The man and woman were talents. I sent them to HQ. There are three more outside. Salome and I will take care of ..."

She was interrupted as the door flew open and three men flew into the room holding pistols. Two were smashed to the floor immediately with thunderbolts from Bret and Bart. A siren started wailing. Esme said in my mind, Suzy, Salome. Throw a shield around the physics package. I did and felt Salome's Add on to mine. The remaining Korean wizard was hit with thunderbolts and he slumped to the floor.

I heard Bret's mental words. "Esme send these three to HQ. All of you gather round the table. I'm taking us home."

And we were standing in the HQ gym, with the package.

Bret said, out loud, "Good work everyone. Now we know the North Koreans have people with talents too. Bart, would you and Salome go get the stuff we left in Seoul and put it here. Esme, would you use you telepathy and talk to our guests. Some may want to stay with us and if so, we'll need to get their families. If not, see what they want to do. See if any of them speak English, please. Suzy, let's go to my place for a minute. Let's meet back here in a half hour, OK." We all nodded and Bret took me to his place.

We kissed like we had been apart a long time. He said, "Suzy, now you've been on an operation with me. They are often like this. Fast grabs with a little fighting and other wizards to worry about. How do you feel now?"

I felt excited and horny. I had heard that violence made girls aroused. I don't think I had ever had that experience before. I noticed my hands were shaking. He looked at them too and said, "That's the adrenaline wearing off. It'll stop in a minute."

I said, "I was excited and when it was over I felt proud. I had contributed to the operation's success. I didn't freeze under the pressure and I didn't wet my pants when the door burst open. Now I'm happy."

He said, "Suzy, I'm proud of you too. You were outstanding, especially for your first operation. I'd be glad to have you along any time."

There's only one way to end an operation like this. I took off my blouse and stepped out of my skirt. He smiled at me and the rest of my clothes as well as his vanished. He carried me into the bedroom and lay me on the bed. I spread my legs as far as I could and put my hands behind my head. I closed my eyes and he touched me, gently. He played me like an organ. I had three starbursts of pleasure before he joined me and the next one was a nova.

Twenty minutes later we were back in the gym with the rest of the team. I realized I was part of the team. It felt great to be a useful part of the team. There was such a feeling of camaraderie. I had never felt this way before.

Esme reported, "None of the five want to go home. Three of them have families we need to rescue ASAP. There is an enclave of over a hundred talents in a school we should get too. All of them speak English. Its a required subject in North Korea."

Bret said, "Good work, Esme. We'll need more bodies for the rescue work. I don't want to go before I talk to the five we picked up. We don't have any idea what kind of defenses to expect. They could be conventional or magical. I'll talk to the boss and get some agents. I want to move everyone at the same time, so we'll need maybe twenty to help us. I think the three of us should go talk to them in person. I'll ask Bart and Salome to listen in and lay a little truth spell of our guests. Everyone OK with that? Neither of us objected. We walked downstairs while Bret talked to Bart.

Bret, Esmerelda and I sat on one side of the table. Four North Korean men and one woman sat on the other side. It was apparent the woman was with one of the men. Esme introduced us. The woman was Bae, the man with her was Chin. The other three men were Cho, Hyun, and Min.

All of them were worried about their families. Their government was holding the talent's families hostage to ensure their good behavior. We had only been back from North Korea for five minutes so our guests thought their families would still be OK. Bret asked about defenses and they all agreed that the defenses were all conventional. They were only trained in teleportation, flight, and use of conventional weapons. Soldiers would take their family members to jail and torture them until they returned. They spoke accented but understandable English.

Bret spread a map on the table. They indicated the school and their families were located on Pujon-ho Lake near Pujon. A hundred students, four hundred family members. More than a thousand soldiers. He told them we were going to go get their families and any others who wanted to leave North Korea. Their smiles of relief were immediate and sincere. Bart asked them if they would like to go and help them find all their family members?

They agreed immediately. Their help would let us get out of there fast and presumably detect any would be infiltrators. They wouldn't be much use if fighting was involved. Since they didn't even know how to make a shield or go invisible. Salome, Esme, and I were invited but all we would be doing was shielding the five defectors. I knew I wasn't much good in a fight and I suspected it was a gender difference. I know Bret and Bart could generate awesome power in the bolts and I couldn't even light a candle yet.

Bret told them we'd leave soon and the three of us went back upstairs. Bart and Salome said they had laid a truth spell on the five and Salome was watching their minds as they talked. She hadn't found any lies.

I took Bret aside and asked if he thought this was safe. I said', "You're planning on taking five hundred people out from under the guns of a thousand troops. Are you sure that twenty five good guys are enough?"

He said, "They have a hard time coming up. Imagine their position. They have to keep us from snatching five hundred folks out of the school. They're up against twenty five flying, invisible, bulletproof wizards that can teleport. By the way, the wizards can put them to sleep or hurl lightning at them. Bart and I will save the lightning in case they try to use artillery or tanks on their prisoners. But the hardest part of their job is going to be explaining to their bosses how they weren't able to stop the exodus with a thousand troops."

Bret assembled the raiders in the gym. We were a motley looking crew, all of us were dressed different. Esme wore a white gown, Salome had her black leather cat suit on. Bart wore his long black leather coat over black pants and shirt. I wore a dark gray t-shirt that said "CUTE BUT CRAZY." All the men save Bart wore jeans and a long sleeve shirt. I guess if you're invisible, bulletproof, fly, and hurl lightning bolts, you don't have to dress for war.

Bret briefed us. He divided us into three teams. Ten men led by Bart, ten more led by him, the women and the five North Koreans. Bart's group was to go to the Army base and teleport all the soldiers there into downtown Pyongyang. His group would find all the soldiers in the school grounds or homes and send them to the same place. The women were to shield the North Koreans. Call for help if they needed it, and locate all the students and families they could. When the men finished moving the soldiers they would relocate the students and families. The men would transport them to an apartment building in Des Moines, Iowa that MG had just purchased. There was room for all the families there. MG was also taking care of US Immigration. There was a secret class of allowed immigrants who were magic users.

Esme, Salome, and I conferred. We agreed we would transport ourselves and our friends to the school. We'd stay invisible and a thousand feet or so above it and to the side in case there were wild shots. We told the North Koreans our plan and they agreed. We could protect innocents from anywhere we could see them.

Chapter 23

Bret said, "Its time folks. Go on three. One..Two..Three" We jumped to the school location and a thousand feet up. We flew a half mile away and watched. It was still. Not a sound. I tuned in to Bret and he was in the school with his men. I didn't talk to him. It seemed all was going well. I watched over his shoulder as he sent two soldiers away. I closed the window and listened to Esme talk to Chin. He was pointing out where his family and Bae's family lived. The others were talking to Salome. All three of us had our shields up and were invisible. I heard a faint noise and saw small lights flying toward us at high speed. I called Bret.

He said, Hi, Suzy. Everything OK?"

"No, there are two airplanes coming toward us, fast."

He said, "OK" and then he was beside me. We watched the planes fly right over the school and two bombs fell off each plane. Bret transported them over the lake. They exploded with enormous fireballs far away over the lake. Bret said, "Airbursts. Large fireballs, probably FAE's."

I asked, "What?"

He explained, "Fuel-Air Explosive. Put some fuel in a tank, blow it all out in a cloud, set off the cloud. Makes a large explosion and would have leveled the school and everyone inside not shielded. Oops."

"I asked, "What Oops?"

He said, "They're coming back, maybe to strafe the buildings since their bombs missed."

Then they disappeared.

"Did you kill them," I asked.

He said, "No. They were just doing their jobs. I just relocated their airplanes a few miles to the East. They shouldn't have any trouble landing, But getting home might involve some paperwork, and their nav systems will likely need some work." I asked, "Right. How many miles?"

He smiled, You're getting to know me too well. About seven hundred. Over Mt. Fuji, Japan.

Salome, Esme and I went to Des Moines to make sure everything went well there. MG had stationed a bunch of people there to sort the families into the correct size apartments. We helped until the mob was tiny then we went back to HQ. The men stayed at the school and made sure we had gotten everyone. Before they left a North Korean wizard appeared in the school looking for his family. Bret sent him to Des Moines. Then all the men came back.

As far as we know it was a perfect operation. No one died and we didn't leave a trace of evidence behind. The North Koreans would want to know what happened or where the people they wanted to keep had gone. And, of course, they lost the nuke they had already paid for.

I was shocked at how little time it took for wizards to plan and execute an operation of two thousand people. It was early afternoon and we had just started this morning. Salome, Esmerelda and I were sitting around Bret's dining table and just killing time. Bret and Bart had gone to Somalia to look into some problem there. They promised to be back for dinner. Bret told me he thought the problem there was a result of some regime change Bart had worked at a few months ago. And by golly he was going to help fix the mess he'd made.

We all had a bottle of beer and some chips. About all I could find in Bret's kitchen. I gathered he didn't cook or eat at home much. I commented, "At least it was clean and tidy."

Esme said, "He doesn't get credit for tidy. There's a cleaning service in all the apartments. The management had to start when it became obvious that hard working wizards and witches left a lot of food out. The rats were getting big enough to scare the familiars."

"You're kidding."

"Exaggerating," she said. "There were a lot of them and the familiars dined well, but still."

236

"So," she asked, "are your rings bothering you now?"

Salome said, "Rings. How do rings bother a witch?"

I said, "I don't want to talk about them."

Salome begged, "Please tell me. I don't know anything about you girls or this place or how I'm going to fit in. I need to know so much."

Esme said, "She's right, Suzy. Its a good story with a cautionary theme for witches. I'll tell her if you don't."

I gave in, "A little while ago I was a psychic detective in Seattle. I found a ring my mother had left that was enchanted, by Asmodeus, I think."

Salome interrupted, "Who's Asmodeus?"

"I read that he's the Demon of Lust and one of the first rank demons in Hell. Powerful. Anyway, I put it on and found I could influence people in matters of the heart. Then I found I couldn't take it off. When all this trouble with Bart took off we thought it might be able to stop him without hurting him. But it wasn't strong enough to affect a person with a talent. Esme and I got the idea we could make it stronger by having a bunch of talents donate power to it. That worked but it changed into a pair of big nipple rings. They were solid gold,> No way to take them out, Besides, they were so strong that if anyone touched one I got an orgasm. Esme touched one and got an orgasm too. She did it a couple of times and we both got huge, mind-blowing orgasms. When I was able to use them to zap Bart into loving you, they've discharged. Now they're back to letting me put spells on non-talented people. They're still enchanted so I can't remove them."

Salome looked impressed and said, "So I can't get an orgasm by touching them? Have you tried anything since zapping Bart?"

"Well, no, but they've stopped doing the other things. When they were charged up, anyone looking at them would give me an orgasm. That's stopped."

Esme said, "Salome's right. We haven't tested them. Show them and let Salome and I try it. The worst that can happen is nothing will happen. If we're lucky all of us will get an orgasm."

Well, I thought, I wouldn't mind an orgasm. I pulled up my T-shirt and pulled down my bra. All three of us looked at them. I said, "use your second sight. "

I turned mine on and saw the fat pink, spaghetti-like strands wrapped around the them. Both girls reached out a hand and flicked a finger against a ring.

I was watching their fingers in scary anticipation. Both hope and dread intermingled in my mind. I saw a bright blue spark jump from the rings, flow up their bodies and disappear in a flash. I had an instant orgasm that threw me back in my chair. My belly spasmed and I felt the love juices flow into my pussy. It was a wonderful surprise. I thought that treat was gone and I had to count on Bret to do it right. But it was huge. Finally, I came up for air and saw both of them sprawled back in their chairs too.

I said, "They must have recharged, girls. That was a fine orgasm. How was yours?"

Esme kind of squeaked, "I..I came but it hurts. Oh No."

"What is it Esme? What happened?"

Salome had slid off the chair and was halfway under the table. I looked down at her and she was holding her breasts tight, like they were trying to escape. She was making a high pitched sound like a high, thin whine.

Esmerelda, was sobbing quietly and tears were running down her cheeks. She kept repeating, "Stupid. Stupid..."

"Esme. Salome. Tell me. What happened?"

Chapter 24

Esmerelda pulled out the top of her gown and looked into her cleavage. She said, "Yup. Just like yours. Just like. Shit on a shingle. I should have known."

I looked inside my shirt, I still had mine.

I asked Salome, "Did you believe my story of the magic nipple rings? I think you just gave yourself a pair. The Doctor can heal them so they don't hurt.

I called up a vision of the Doctor. "Doc, can you come to Bret's apartment. I have two girls here who need a healer."

After the Doctor had left I took off my top. I went to both the shocked women and bared their breasts so we could see each other. "Girls, these rings never replicated before. Esme has touched them and so has Bret. Esme and I get orgasms when she touches them. Bret gives me an orgasm but doesn't feel anything himself. Does the pink color of the enchantment mean it only works on girls?

Esme said, "Yes, spells can be gender specific. Pink for girls, blue for boys, any other color for either. That's how pink and blue got associated with girls and boys."

I went on, "We can simply adjust to having them and not let anyone touch them or we can work on a better solution. What do you want?"

Salome said, "I want to get rid of them."

Esme said, "Me too."

I said, Esme, you're most familiar with how magic works. What shall we do?"

She said, Magic and enchantments are tricky. Sometimes they can evolve from the original as events and the environment changes. Just a minute. Her eyes changed and then went back to normal. Suzy, your rings are no longer enchanted and neither is Salome's. Only mine are enchanted."

I turned on my second sight and confirmed what she reported.

She said, Both of you can probably remove your rings now, if you want."

Salome looked down and her rings disappeared.

I looked at mine and said, "I've grown fond of them. Since now they seem to be just gold rings, I think I'll keep them for a while."

Esme asked, "Suzy, I hate to ask, but would you see if the enchantment comes home if you touch my rings?"

I was startled. "What? You want to give the curse back to me? Why Should I?"

"I know its a lot to ask, but we need to find out how they work. Will the enchantment just trade witches whenever we touch? Will it stay in me because it was in you so long? Will the touch of someone who already has rings nullify the curse? Will it refuse to go back into you because you have a lover?"

Salome said, "I need another beer. Anyone else?"

I said, "Not a beer. I need something stronger. There's a bottle of single malt in the cupboard over the sink. Would you get me that and a glass.?"

Esme said, "Two glasses. please."

Salome got the bottle and three glasses. She poured three doubles. I sipped, then threw back my head and sucked it down. Salome and Esme looked at me and copied me. Salome poured another glass each. Now I was ready to sip.

Esme said, "This may be our best opportunity to learn how these rings work."

I looked at Salome and said to myself sotto voce, "Salome you've drunk my beer, now touch her rings and be a dear."

It worked, Salome reached out and touched one of Semi's rings. Both girls looked shocked and both girls had an instant orgasm. When I looked both girls had rings and both were enchanted. Oh my. I hadn't thought that would happen. I felt bad for both of them. I decided they didn't need to know what I had done.

I said, My gosh, Salome. Why did you do that? Did the ring summon you?"

Salome looked a little dazed. She said, I..I don't know why. I just had to do it. It was like watching someone else's hand reach out. It must have been the rings."

Esme must have seen the lie in my face. She said, "Suzy, if you had said a love ring spell under your breath, it would have had the same effect, wouldn't it?"

I thought about how to respond. I'm not a good liar so I temporized. "But Esme, now that the rings are discharged, they aren't strong enough to work on a talent."

Esme smiled a rather cynical smile and said, "Yes, that's what we thought wasn't it. We should test that. "

I couldn't think of a thing to say or do but shake my head, silently pleading.

Esme slowly said, "Suzy, if you had Salome touch my ring then you must do the same."

I couldn't help myself. My hand reached out and touched Semi's ring and I was flung back into my chair by my spasming body. The orgasm was enormous and it lasted for a long time. My belly was clenching and releasing, pumping my love juices onto my chair. When Esme and I were done, all three of us has the pink spaghetti around our nipple rings.

When we recovered, I looked at them and said, "I'm sorry, Salome. I wasn't thinking."

She replied, "OK. Accepted. I don't think any of us is thinking straight now. You two just had a nice orgasm, are you still feeling a little aroused? I only ask because I am so hot right now. I want to go get Bart and spend the rest of the day playing 'Hide the sausage.'"

I took stock of my feelings and said, "Me too. The rings are up to full charge again."

Esme, "Yeah. I'm horny too, but I don't have a current boyfriend."

I said, "Esmerelda, you're a hot bitch. You can find a willing partner in 2 minutes. I saw the Doctor eyeing you when he was here."

"I had two big gold rings stuck into my breasts. Of course he looked at me."

"OK," I said, looking at her pointedly, "Esmerelda, you know its late, so go ask the Doctor for a date."

Esmerelda, stood up, closed her gown, said, "Shit," and walked out of the apartment.

I turned to Salome and asked, 'So, before you became Sauron's minion, what did you do?"

She looked defiantly back at me and said, "I taught school."

"Really, where and what ages?"

I taught high school in San Diego. History. That's when I learned I had some magic in me."

"What happened?"

I was at home watching a movie on DVD. It was a Chinese Martial Arts picture. Crouching Tiger, Hidden Dragon.' People were sailing around in he trees and I found myself floating above my chair. I only realized it when I bumped into the ceiling. I found I could fly just by visualizing myself flying. I played around with it for a couple of years. I got a broomstick for show and would give the kids a thrill on Halloween. One day Bart/Sauron found me and he convinced me to give up my mundane life for some adventure. How about you?"

I said, "I found I could make visions appear of people and things. I opened a PI office in Seattle. Soon I was known as the Psychic PI. I made a decent living finding lost or stolen things for people. The occasional felon the police wanted back, missing people. Then I found this ring my mother left. I put it on and well, it let's me cast spells. Then I was looking for a missing defendant and I got a vision of Bret instead. I think that was the ring's doing. Don't get me wrong. Bret and MG are the best things that ever happened to me. But the rings are playing me to their tune. I'm just a passenger most of the time. You and Esme are the collateral damage to the ring's twisting my life around. I'm, We're helpless passengers on its trip. If it wants me to get pregnant, I don't think little pink pills will stop it."

"I understand your feelings. I just acquired some of them too," Salome said, "but it sounds like you've gained a lot from the ring."

"Yeah, and I'm grateful. Magic, Bret, becoming a team asset. I still feel like Asmodeus is watching me and screwing with my head. He is a demon, after all. Speaking of demons of lust, my arousal is intense. My pussy is tingling and my belly is filling me with love juice. I need Bret now. How do you feel?"

She said, "The same. I'm about to burst. I don't think its wise for us to touch each other's rings now. I'm afraid we'd both wind up worse off. Nose rings or labia rings or a gold collar saying 'Love Me,' or worse."

I said, "Those are delightful thoughts, Salome. I think you're right, though. No touching. Shall we call the boys? They must be about done. Its almost five. I have a promise from Bret to take me back to those exotic cities and fancy hotels. Want a double date tonight? Dinner and a hotel in, say, Casablanca? Maybe a triple date if Esmerelda got lucky?"

Salome said, sounds good. You call Bret, I'll call Esme."

I thought about Bret and he answered immediately. I thought, "Hi, Love. I am missing you terribly. My rings are driving me horny again. Can you come home now?"

Bret's voice rang in my mind, "Great timing. Everything is wrapped up here and it was Bart. Bye."

Bret and Bart appeared in the room. Both Salome and I still had our breasts bared and the guys smiled. Bart said, "You got rings like Suzy. They look good on you."

Salome dimpled and I said, "Boys, these are recharged love rings. Don't touch one with your skin until you're ready for us to orgasm. It'll happen as soon as they're touched. We have dinner plans and need to love you first. So let's go."

I flew into Bret's arms and Salome into Bart's. We kissed for a long time before Bret jumped us into the bedroom. I don't think Bart waited because I heard Salome's scream of pleasure before I was undressed. Our clothes slithered off us and floated into the closet. Bret asked, "What do you prefer tonight Suzanne? Flying over the forest like eagles mating in flight? Missionary position? Doggy style? Would you like to be on top?"

I said, Today I was reclaimed by the rings. Finish the job. Put me in bondage and ravish my helpless body. Tonight, in this room, I am your salve and you are my master."

Bret said, "Kinky. Alright. Something new. The bed slid over six feet and an oak pillory appeared on the floor. He opened the heavy bar and invited me to position my neck and wrists in the semicircular slots. I placed my neck in the cold, hard wood. I pulled my hair to my right side and placed my hands in their slots. Bret lowered the locking bar in place and locked it down with a loud click. He pulled my left foot out and tied it there. Then my right foot was tied so I was spread wide open. I felt my labia lips separate so my inner lips were exposed to the cool breeze. He let me stand there for a few moments.

I felt the heavy rings swaying and tugging my breasts down and side to side. I was so horny. I begged him, "Please master, take your slave. Your slave needs you in her. I beg to submit to you, Master. Please take me."

I wiggled my ass, about the only movement I was able to make. I hoped it would inflame him to take me. He rubbed his hands over my bottom. He was so close to my pussy. If he'd only touch me there I could come, I know it. He said, " I love the way your ass moves. Its so inviting."

"Please master take me in my ass of my cunt. You're my master. Please take some way, now. I'm so needy."

Bret said, "You're awfully demanding for my slave girl. I suppose I could gag you or maybe you'd like to service me with your mouth?"

I yelled, "Yes, master, Let me service you, Please, Master."

I saw him saunter around the side of the pillory and his cock was rampant. He looked huge and I wanted him. He got close enough and I licked and kissed the tip of his penis. I was hungry for more, but I couldn't move my head. The yoke was tight and unyielding.

He moved closer and thrust his cock into me It was yummy. It tasted like he smelled. This was the most submissive act a woman could perform on a man. Intercourse was fine and we had to submit for that too. It was a woman's lot in life to submit to man. But this was the most subjugating act. When I invited him into my mouth, I was giving up everything. I would obey him in all things forever. Far too soon he came in me and filled my throat and mouth with his salty spend. I swallowed it all, every drop, and swallowed all my pride with it.

He pulled out and walked around me, rubbing his hand down my back. He stopped be side me and lowered his hand to fondle my breast. He was gentle, too gentle. I asked, "Please master, don't be gentle with me. I want you to be rough. Make me feel your power."

He said, "Be quiet, woman."

"Yes, Master."

He slapped my breast, not hard enough, but I didn't dare say anything more. I had a command to obey. Then he touched my ring. My orgasm was immediate and huge. I screamed in pleasure. I fought my bonds but they were far stronger than I. I made my breasts sway and my ass move, but that was all. I clenched my fists in helpless reaction to my spasming belly. I felt my love juices flowing out of my pussy and down my legs. I felt so empty. My orgasm was strong and very pleasant but I missed my partner, my master in me. I gasped and moaned and as I stilled, I asked, "Master please fuck me. I need you inside me so badly. The orgasm you gave me was wonderful, but its the icing on my missing cake. Please take me as a man takes his woman.

H came back to my head and said, "Open wide. I did as he ordered and he slipped a ball gag in my mouth and tightened the strap behind my head. He said, I need to recharge. I'll be back in a while."

I yelled, "No, I can make you hard again." Which of course was completely unintelligible." I tried to open a vision to him, but I couldn't get through. Rats. My need for him was huge. I moaned in frustration and tried every contortion I could manage, but nothing helped.

I relived every encounter I had had with the most masculine man I had ever known. He had tantalized me, driven me to orgasm the very first time I saw him in that fight in the jungle. I was right. He was Conan. He was so much more than any other man. Even before the rings he drove me to orgasm with the gentlest of touches. His image drove me to astounding heights of arousal. Now, today, I was his slave girl by my own gift. His to do with as he pleased. I felt an erotic excitement in his ownership of me. I had no choices at all. My feelings and desires were of no concern to anyone, even me. It was a silly romantic fantasy probably borne by the rings, but I wished he would claim me for his own. That same fantasy had made me ask to have her collar and shackles retained.

Someday she might find a way he could keep them on me, his real slave girl.

After a long, boring, frustrating time, I heard him return. Then I felt his cock nuzzling at my sopping wet pussy. I shoved my ass as far back as I could, which was not very far . His cock thrust in a little so he touched my inner lips. I tried to open them more, but my feet were tied solid and I couldn't move anything useful. He teased me as I cursed him through my gag. He was making my need worse. He was touching me but staying outside. I needed him in me so bad. My guts were twisting and clenching, trying to feel him. To get some relief. I was one huge itch inside. I needed him. Finally he slid into me and I felt such relief as my body accepted it was being fucked.

He slid in and out and I was near to an orgasm when he reached down and took both of my nipple rings in his hands. I had an instant orgasm. It was outstanding to orgasm with him in me. But he didn't release me. My orgasm started to subside and my squeals died down when another one hit me. I wasn't ready. It wasn't a surprise, exactly, but it literally drove the breath out of me. I screamed and screamed through my gag. In the end I was limp and still spasming inside.

He released my rings after he orgasmed and I had had maybe ten in a row. He pulled out and took the gag out of my mouth. He asked, "Was it as good as you hoped?"

I said, weakly, "Better, master, better. But I may have to give up sex for a day. I'm wasted."

He untied my legs and raised the bar. He helped me stand up and we kissed.

I felt the massive oak pillory and wondered, "Where did you get this?"

"I made it for you. Did I mention wizards are good at making things."

"What are you going to do with it now?"

He said, I can get rid of it or store it somewhere, or leave it here for later. Your choice?"

I thought about doing this all again soon. I said, "Let's keep it a while. Its a good conversation piece."

He said, "All right. I guess this means I'm your master as long as its here."

"Don't push your luck buddy. What happens in the bedroom stays in the bedroom."

Bret smiled, and agreed, "Sounds fair. I'm looking forward to trying it out again. I think I need to work on y technique."

"Your technique is just fine, buddy boy. Now you promised me we'd go back to some of those exotic cities for a visit. Would you take me, Salome, and Esme and their dates to Casablanca? Dinner and a stay in that fancy hotel we visited for ten minutes a few days ago?"

"Sure. Esme has a boyfriend?"

I said, "Maybe the Doctor. We'll see. Let's get dressed and I want something nice."

He asked, How about the clothes you had on our first dinner. They haven't seen them and I thought you looked wonderful in them."

I remembered that magical evening and I agreed, "But," I said, "the other girls have to look just as good. "He looked at me, thoughtfully and said, "Nope. Impossible. They'll have to settle for 'Almost as good.'"

"Thank you, master. And that's the last time I call you master tonight."

"We'll see," he said.

I usually didn't bother, but I did like to dress up and look nice. I guess now that I looked like a real girl I enjoyed it more. The lust radiating from the men was great, but the envy from the other women was even better. Of course I didn't know if it was my looks or my Manolo Blahnik high heeled, blue, 'Fuck Me' pumps they envied more.

Esmerelda did hook up with the Doctor, All six of us met in Bret's living room. He got us three Grand Deluxe suites in the Riad Jnane Sherazade. All he would say about the cost was that they were over three thousand a night and the US Government was glad to furnish them to us for returning their nukes to them. We were booked in for a week. Salome and Esme looked almost as good as me (hah). and the boys all had custom tuxedos. We ate in a fine, elegant restaurant called Asador Coto Real. They had excellent beef and I wanted to go back and try some of their other goodies later in our stay. We all played tourist after dinner. We didn't have to change and transportation wasn't a problem. We split up into three pairs (guess who) and flew invisibly all over the city. I'm just a girl at heart, I guess. My favorite place was the Sinbad Park. It was like an Arabian Disneyland with a zoo. I made Bret go to every exhibit with me. He was quite tolerant of my childlike exuberance over the animals. With our invisibility and shields and flight, we could see things no one not so equipped could. The big cats smelled and heard us, but left us alone.

We went back to the hotel together then split up, agreeing to meet for breakfast at 10. Bret and I went to our t=room the conventional way, via the elevator. When we got in out room he put my clothes in the closet and changed into some casual slacks and polo shirt.

I asked, "What am I getting to wear?"

He said, "something you liked before and asked me to save for you." The steel collar materialized on my neck followed by the shackles on my ankles.

"Hey, no fair. I'm not your slave girl any more."

"No? I think you want to be sometimes. If I'm wrong, tell me and I'll change your steel attire to standard clothing. Otherwise, tonight you are my property. Call me master as long as you wear my collar." I was formulating a loving but scathing reply when he walked up to me and took hold of a nipple ring.

My orgasm was immediate. I started to collapse when he took me in his arms and held me. It was so good. I wanted him in me, but being held by him was a close second. When my writhing subsided, he set me down and asked, "Do you want to be my slave girl tonight?

I grabbed him and jumped into his arms again, "Damn right I do, Master."

We played for hours. I gave him a couple of good orgasms. Between his magic finger, his stiff member, and my enchanted rings, I had at least ten.

Chapter 25

In the morning we played some more in bed then showered. He left the collar and shackles on me while we showered and dressed. After we got dressed we looked like middle class tourists. Except I still wore my slave collar and shackles.

I asked, "I'm going to be a little conspicuous with this hardware, aren't I, Master?"

He said, "I don't think so. It goes well with your coloring and clothes. Look in the mirror."

I walked over in front of the mirror and I didn't see the collar but I still felt it. I looked down at the shackles. They were invisible too. I said, "I didn't know you could make something I'm wearing invisible without making me invisible too."

He just smiled and said, "Remember, its 'Master' while you wear them."

"Master, I asked, invisible or not, that chain going to make a lot of noise when I walk."

He said, "I can fix that." He stood me on top of a table and fiddled with the shackles. He set me back on the floor and said, walk to the door and back. I looked down, but they were invisible. I found the chain was quiet but my stride was shorter. He said, I shortened the chain so it won't hit the floor and coated it with plastic so it won't clatter." Its long enough you can climb standard stairs. I wouldn't try and run in them though."

I protested, "You're not wearing them. Its so short I can't keep up with you when you walk."

He was not a bit sympathetic, "Slaves make do with what they're given. I've given you a short stride. Take shorter steps faster. Or fly. Or decide you don't want to be my property," he smirked.

"Can the others see my collar and shackles?"

"Not unless they look at you with their second sight, and then, only Bart is strong enough to see my spell. The others won't see them. Unless I let them."

I said, "Please don't do that, master. I'm your slave and I'll do whatever you order, but I'm not ready for others to know that. I would be too embarrassed."

We joined the others for breakfast in the hotel's restaurant. I knew they couldn't see my bondage. It didn't help much. I knew it was there. Bret knew it was there. Before this I had been a leader among the women. I would have ideas and suggest things to do or approaches to take. Not now. I was submissive and always agreed with everyone else. Just before lunch, Esme asked me about it. She asked, Suzy, are you feeling All right?"

"I feel fine, Esme."

"You haven't said a word all day. Its like you've suddenly turned shy and retiring. That's not the Suzy I've come to know. You always have ideas and you never just say 'OK' to Bret. Has he been mean to you?"

"Oh no, Esme. He's always been a perfect gentleman and listens to my ideas. I'm trying to be less aggressive. I used to scare people off. I think I was a PI too long and I'm trying to change." What I meant was I wanted Bret to keep me and I didn't care how he did it. I guess this was me trying to convince him to stay loyal to me despite all the choices he had. I'm sure there were other beautiful women who would like to he his wife, or girlfriend. I didn't think there would be as many who would accept being his slave girl if he was faithful to her. Today was a kind to test of my resolve, at least for me. I wasn't sure about Bret.

Thankfully we mostly flew around Morocco to see the sights rather than walking. I was sure Esme would see my strained gait if I had to walk far when she was around. She seemed to be the most observant one. Except Bret. I saw him watching me all the time. He seemed to like what he saw. Just the addition of the invisible steel changed my personality. I thought like his slave all day. I got him things before he asked. I watched him for the slightest sign of wanting something or for me to do something. I stayed three paces behind him and to his right. I was heeling him without any training. It was just the best place for me to see what he wanted as a soon as I could. Whenever he stopped I stopped beside him and put my hand in his. It was some kind of wonderful having him so close all day, even if my only goal was his pleasure. To my mind this is love. The knowledge that your love's happiness is essential to your own.

After dinner that night he took the steel off me. I felt lost. I was safe when I wore his steel. I had gotten used to it and I knew what was expected of me. Without it I was a full human again with all my rights and responsibilities renewed. I didn't know how to do that anymore. My collar and shackle provided a certainty, a boundary to stay inside. When I was free, my world was too big. I sat in Bret's lap and asked, "Master, what should I do?"

"Suzy, he said, "I'm not your master now. I'm your lover and friend."

"Yes, master." I want to be more than your friend."

"I know. I want you as my friend always. I need your love whenever I can. I can't own a slave. I have nowhere to keep you, nor anyone to look after you when I'm gone. My job is necessary and I can't leave it until I have a qualified replacement. With some more training you could be my partner, but not yet. You need to go back to your life in Seattle. You have employees and friends who need you. I will visit whenever I can, and that means I'll probably be in your bed more than half the time."

I cried for too long. I knew he was right. I couldn't ask him to leave his job and I couldn't go with him yet. I needed to go home and make sure Gus and Millie get paid and Lynn has a place to live. And I missed them.

I would have to come back to HQ and learn how to do so many wonderful things. Already Gus and I can completely revamp the business. I said, "Bret, I'm yours forever. Whenever you want me, come to Seattle and I'll obey you and give you the most pleasure I can. I'll be faithful to you. I can't be anything but your property now. You own me, even if you're an absentee landlord. Your property will always welcome you with open arms. I won't let anyone but you touch my rings. You are my master. Now take me to bed and make this vacation last forever."

We stayed the rest of the week in Casablanca. But we went all over the region. Ten countries. Teleports have so much more time to use productively. We jumped all over the near east and never entered an airport or were asked for identification. Oh, there were a couple of times where a cop stopped us to ask who we were. Bret sent them to the far side of the city and we never answered them. Four times unsuspecting locals tried to rob us wealthy tourists. That didn't work out so well for them. Once we were standing on an overlook into a lush valley. A truckload of heavily armed men roared up beside us waving their weapons in the air. Bret and Bart sent their weapons into the Red Sea and questioned them. They were simple bandits that saw us as targets of opportunity. They were sent on the way without their weapons. No harm, no foul.

I thought about me and Bret a lot. We were intimate in a way I had never known before. We were perfect, physically. But this was more than physical. We were connected so deeply I could feel his soul. Being able to find someone you click with so naturally is the best feeling ever. I felt like we've been best friends our whole life, it felt like coming home. I'm so comfortable with him. Maybe that's what a soulmate is. Not someone who shares every single thing in common with you, but someone who feels like home. I knew I was home with him.

I couldn't make him be faithful to me. I thought he would be. But I could show my faithfulness to him. I got on the internet and found a company that made fetish gear of stainless steel. I called them and explained what I wanted. They were confused by my request, but would do it for money. I gave them my credit card information and paid extra for overnight delivery. My package arrived at the hotel in two days. I took it into the bath with me, alone and opened the package. It was gleaming and perfect. I took it back into the living room and showed it to Bret. "I had this made for me to wear. What do you think?"

He held the shiny thing up and read the inscription," PROPERTY OF BRET THORNE."

He looked at me. It is solid. It doesn't open."

"That's right. I knew a wizard of your skill could tell that right away. Put it on me, please."

He said, "Well, it that's what you want. I am honored."

The collar settled on my neck, halfway up and snug. Just where I wanted it. The silver ring dangled from its staple. If I raised my chin the ring bumped my neck. I kissed him.

"I don't want this made invisible. I want the world to know," I said, "whenever you're with me, you're my Master.

Salome and Esmerelda were properly appreciative. I told them I could get them one of their own when they were ready.

Chapter 26

When the week was over we all went home. Esmerelda and the Doctor went back to HQ. Esmerelda said he made excellent use of her new rings and she would never be lonely again.

Bret and I went to HQ for a brief training session. Jason taught me how to jump to Bret and HQ. That was all I needed for now. I promised to go back to HQ for more lessons and set up a weekly session with him. Then we came back to my house in Seattle on a Wednesday afternoon. I called Millie and Gus. They were at the office and said they were doing OK. Gus had closed several old cases and they had two new ones for me. I told them I'd be in tomorrow.

"I feel I should do something with the new abilities Gus and I got from MG," I told Bret.

"Like what?"

"Gus wants to open a bail bond company. He thinks its a waste for him to find the skip and then have to give half the finder's fee to someone who takes the skip in."

He asked, "What do you think?"

"Its complex. First, I don't have the money to write a bunch of bonds, now. Second, I don't want to put any of the existing bondsmen out of business using magic. Their employees need to earn a living. And third, I like being the 'Psychic PI.'"

He asked, "Are there any people the existing bondsmen don't serve?"

'Yes. Of course. Some poor folks can't afford the fee. Some the bail is too high because of flight risk or danger to the community, or just because its a high profile case."

He said, "With your abilities and your new friends, and your rings, you can help some of those folks. The poor, the innocent, even those who are a flight risk. They could never run out on you."

"Even so, no money."

He smiled and said, "About that. The government knows the key role you played in getting their nukes back. They have shown their gratitude." He pulled a folded piece of paper out of his shirt pocket and handed it to me.

I unfolded it. It was a check with a lot of zeros. A cool million dollars. I looked at all the writing. It was from a Swiss bank and drawn on the account of Bret Thorne.

"Bret, this is from you, not the government."

"MG doesn't want any government to know who their talented people are. I'm the front man for many governments that need magic assistance, so they all know me. It all goes in my name and the bank we use id owned by MG so they never, never tell any government the whole truth. This would be a big deposit for you so, you have an account set up in our bank. They will keep your transactions private if you want. Call Heinrik and he'll get you set up." He gave me a business card.

I thought about what he said. I smelled a rat. This was too smooth. "Did you just think up all this about my business?"

"Well, it was mostly mine, especially, convincing them to give me money for one of my key operatives. But I got a little help."

"Come clean Bret Thorne. Who else is involved?"

"Esme. Salome. Bart. Gus. Millie. Lucifer"

"Lucifer? He's a cat."

Bret smiled again, "No. Lucifer is a familiar. He looks like a cat. He knows your mind and business better than you do. He had to in order to protect you properly. I've talked to him and some others of his kind. They don't just attach themselves to anyone. He was assigned to you. His only duty is your protection. There are some entities not kindly disposed toward you and others like you. He would be an excellent being on which to practice telepathy."

I asked, "So, they just want to see me succeed here?"

He said, "You know, Suzy, you have a lot of insight in your beautiful head. No. They want to be a part of your operation if you can make it interesting."

"What? All of them? What kind of operation do they want me to have?"

"Esme just wants some part time gigs. She's enamored of the Doctor at HQ, but she can be here in an instant, as you well know."

"And the others?"

"You know what Gus wants. The thrill of the chase. Bart wants to be active and make Salome happy. Salome wants to help the underdog. I think Millie just wants a bigger paycheck."

Now the important question. "How about you? Will you help out too?"

He said, "Think of me as your enforcer. Your strong right hand. If you ever need me, just call. Other times I'll lend a sympathetic ear and all the moral support I have."

"I'm about ready for some moral support now."

We retired to my boudoir and he tweaked my rings. Boy, does that phrase have a new meaning now. When we finished and I recovered, I called Heinrik and set up my account. Bret handed me a thin checkbook drawn on a numbered account. "If you want to write a check over fifty thousand, call Heinrik first."

I called Lynn and told her the danger was gone and she was welcome to come back.

She said, she'd be back tonight. "I can't stand it here. My parents are good people but I can't live with them any more."

I asked, "Do you need any help moving your things?" I knew Mack had moved five boxes and a suitcase of her 'Essentials' when I sent her home.

"God, yes. The sooner the better. My stuff is still in boxes so I'm ready to go. "

OK. My friend is in the neighborhood. I'll ask him to get to your place ASAP."

I turned to Bret, "Would you mind?"

"What's the address?"

I gave it to him. Clothes appropriate to Seattle appeared on him. (Gore-Tex jacket with hood, cargo pants and hiking boots) He said, "When in Rome..." and vanished.

Minutes later he reappeared. And changed back into the shorts and T-shirt he'd been wearing before. "She's driving her car back. I told her to leave and I'd put her things in my truck after she left. I put her things in her room. I didn't show her any magic, but I think she saw some when this started. Handle her however you want, but remember loose lips may get the feds interested. We may help them, but they would love to control us. They're always trying to find out who 'We' are."

Lynn came in about an hour later. Her folks live in Auburn so she must have come directly here. She did a double take when she saw Bret. "Hey. I broke the speed limit all the way here. How did you beat me?"

Bret smiled and replied, "My truck is disguised as an ambulance. I parked it down the street. You must have come in the other way."

Lynn said, "I didn't see any ambulance on the street," and walked to the window.

Bret shook his head and Lynn walked back to us. "Sorry, I see it now." She turned to me and hugged me "Gosh, its good to see you Suzy. Tell me what happened. And tell me about your new necklace. A bit Goth, but it is about time you stepped out of the mold."

I said, "Just like I told you before. I saw the killer as he took out the guy I was looking for. I found the killer's photo in their mug shots and the caught him and his gang. They got enough evidence they don't need me anymore. I won't be a witness since I only saw him in my vision, I'm home free and so are you. Oh, and this gentleman is Bret Thorne. He's with the FBI and we've kind of hooked up. He'll be an extra level of security when he's here. I looked at Bret, "And I hope he's here a lot.

I went on, "Yeah, about the necklace. Its not removable. I fell for Bret pretty hard. I had it made and put on me permanently. He didn't ask me for that. It was all my idea. I decided there was no point

268

in pussyfooting around. I'm his and I don't want to ever be anyone else's. He has to travel a lot and its my way of telling him I intend to be faithful when he's gone."

Lynn said, "Wow, that's pretty romantic. Thorne, you'd better marry Suzy real soon. Can I touch it?"

"Sure, Lynn."

She touched it with her right hand and tugged on the ring. She said, "It feels like the real thing. You can't take it off?"

"Never. Walk around and look at it closely. There's no key, no hidden latches, no hinges. Its not coming off unless its cut."

Lynn repeated herself, "Wow. You're either the bravest or dumbest broad in Seattle. Maybe both. Or maybe you're something else entirely."

"Yep. I'm sure I'm one of those. Now its late, your stuff is in your room. Bret and I are going to bed and ignore any noises you hear. I need a good spanking."

I took Bret's hand and we went up to my bedroom.

Once I closed the door, I whispered in Bret's ear, "bend me over, slide it in and own me."

In the morning I threw the sheets in the hamper and made a note to get a rubber pad for the bed. I was going to have to replace this mattress. We were certainly messy.

Bret had some wizard stuff to do so he dropped me at the office, said hello to Millie and Gus, and left.

I locked the front door and had a conference with Gus and Millie. I started, "Bret tells me you've been talking to him about some improvements you'd like to see."

Millie said, "I hope you're not mad, boss. He seemed interested in helping us."

"No, of course not. You see my collar. I consider myself his property. Anything I have is really his. When he's around, I want him to make all the decisions. Now tell me what we should be doing. Assume we have all the money in the world."

Gus said, "OK, boss. I think we should do bail bonds. Those guys get ten percent on their money and with our abilities we'll never lose a skip."

Uh Oh. "Millie do you know what Gus means by 'Our abilities?'"

She said, "Not really. Since he's come back, he talks about how easy it is to follow skips and he's made a bunch of collars for the bail guys. What's going on?"

I was very lucky. I hadn't cautioned Gus about talking. Good thing he was a former special operator. Those guys never talked about what, where, or when they did anything. I said, "Gus and I got trained on some new secret surveillance gear and we swore never to talk about it. Right, Gus?"

Gus said, "Right, boss."

I said, "OK, Gus. Bail bonds. Anything else?"

He said, "I bet we would be good at regular PI stuff as well as your Psychic specialty. We'd need more people though."

I said, "OK, bail bonds and regular PI work. Millie?"

She said, "I like both those ideas. I don't have anything else. If you're going to get more people or do bonds, you're going to need a bookkeeper and more space."

"Good. I understand. I like the bail bonds idea, but I want to find a customer base that's not being served now. I'm thinking of the poor folks can't afford a bond now. The high profile cases where the bail's too high and the flight risks. I also met some more people who might help us. They're from the same place we got our surveillance training , Gus. I'll bring them by tomorrow."

Gus nodded his approval.

I unlocked the front door and was walking back to my office when I heard it burst open and a baying like the hounds of hell. I threw up my shield and heard a THUD behind me. Horus was sitting on the floor two feet away. Father Magnus was running toward me followed by Sister John Hancock. Gus stepped in front of Magnus and said in his calm voice, "Stop." His calm voice is the one that makes the people he speaks to take a step back.

Father Magnus said, "She is possessed. I must exorcise the demon Asmodeus from her body. Her soul is in peril. No harm will befall her if I can exorcise the demon. Let me by."

He might be right. It might be Asmodeus in my rings. They were enchanted. If he can get rid of Asmodeus, or at least the enchantment, I won't be forced into an orgasm when they're touched. Not that I mind orgasms, but I want Bret in me when I have them. Much more sociable . Besides, I don't much like having anyone else telling my body what to do.

Gus said, "Out and take your friend and dog with you."

I said, "Gus, wait a minute. Father Magnus, how do you make a demon leave."

Father Magnus said, It only takes a minute. I have to just order the demon to leave and cite the religious authority. He must leave then."

"Well, OK then. Gus, escort our visitors to my office, please."

I sat at my desk, Magnus stood in front of me, Sister John Hancock stood behind me and Gus stood behind Father Magnus. Horus had recovered and was licking my right shoe. I said, "OK, Father, do it."

He started chanting something in Latin. Finally he switched to English and said, "I order you to leave this person in the name of the Father, the Son, and the Holy Spirit."

That must have done it. I didn't feel any different, but Sister John Hancock yelled "Asmodeus" and ran out of the room. Horus looked confused and stopped licking my shoe. He raised his head, looked at the open door and ran out just as I heard my front door slam. Father Magnus ran after them and I yelled, "Thanks and good luck. Gus shook his head and followed them out. I pulled my blouse out far enough to see my nipple rings and turned on my second sight. Just gold rings. No pink spaghetti strands. I was free. Just to be sure I looked all around my office and inside my desk with my second sight. Clean. No trace of a spell anywhere. I turned it off.

I surmised that the exorcism worked and Asmodeus jumped into Sister John Hancock.

I tried for a vision of the sister and found her. She was inside the topless bar across pioneer square from my office. I looked for Father Magnus. The bouncer outside was having none of Father Magnus protests and wouldn't let him in. Horus was at the door licking it. I switched back to the sister. She had doffed her collar and headdress. She was in the manager's office negotiating for more money. The manager was losing the battle and staring at the sister's now quite impressive breasts. Asmodeus' work, undoubtedly. I closed the vision and looked back at my impressive breasts and said, "Thank you Asmodeus. Now stay away, please."

Chapter 27

It turns out that I added a new skill to MG's repertoire. Before me, no one could use visions to find things. Its hard to teach too. In exchange for teaching me how to teleport I agreed to teach them how to do my vision thing. I only had limited success. There seems to be some limitations on who a person can teach. Only case like this they know of, but, its a big world. Bigger for me than it used to be. I was able to teach Bret, but that's all. Most of that happened in bed, so that may be part of the method. Bret was able to teach Bart and Esmerelda. Common genes? Bart taught Salome. Sex? Bed?

Esmerelda's trying to teach the Doctor, and they're still an item. I don't know if she's succeeded yet.

I told Esme and Salome how to get rid of the ring's enchantment but they've kept them so far.

I opened PPI Bail Bonds with Bret's help. He has a lot of pull with all the government's involved. PPI stands for Psychic PI and we only write bonds none of the others will touch. We never forfeit a bond.

PPI Bail Bonds and Psychic Private Investigations share a staff and offices . My new friends joined the firm as partners. Bart and Gus do most of the field work, pickups, retrievals, surveillance. They love it. Salome and Esme are in charge of interrogations. No one can lie to them. Everyone but Millie and her new bookkeeper/assistant use visions to find people and things.

Sometimes things go awry in a big way and our skills are able to straighten them out.

Bart and Salome had been together for three months and it became quite apparent that she was pregnant. She assured me it was planned and Bart was happy with the changes in their lives. Salome had been house shopping and she found one she liked. It was in the million dollar range, so she should like it. It was larger on a big lot with a view of the water and mountains. She didn't have any credit history. Schoolteachers turned evil wizard's minion don't usually. MG was providing her with the cash and I was with her in our bank getting some forms notarized. We were in a loan officer's windowed office. A burst of automatic gunfire shattered the calm environment. There were women's screams and men yelling amid the shattering of falling glass. We raised our shields wide enough to protect the notary and looked out the window into chaos. Men with assault rifles were fanning out from the front door and a guard lay bleeding on the floor. I got Bart and Gus on a mental link and told them what was happening. Bart brought Gus with him into the office. Salome put the loan officer to sleep and she collapsed to the floor.

Bart said, "The guard was shot several times. His heart's stopped. I'll send him to HQ. The guard vanished. Bart replaced him with a clothes manikin

276

from the store front across the street. I noticed the manikin was now dressed as a bank guard,

"Nice work, Bart."

He said, "I take pride in my work, Suzy."

"Can you tell how many robbers are here?"

Bart said, "There are eight guy with guns in this room and two more downstairs."

A gunshot came faintly. and Bart said, "Be right back."

He disappeared and reappeared seconds later. "Two bad guys unconscious in the vault now. They shot the manager after he opened the vault. I sent him to HQ medical. Want the other robbers dead or gone?"

I thought a moment. "No. Salome, make all the ones you can see fall asleep." I dug a handful of Psychic PI cards out of my purse and handed them to Gus. "Gus, go make all the other's unconscious in a more conventional way and lay one of these card on all of them. Bart, see if anyone else needs medical car at HQ or if they can be fixed in Seattle. Send the serious ones to HQ. And bring back the ones HQ is done with. Get rid of the manikin then. When all that's done, Bart, take Salome down to the vault. Wake the crooks up and find out if there's anyone not here who's responsible."

I handed Salome a couple of cards and said, "Make sure they have our calling cards too. Now go."

I watched the chaos outside my window resolve itself. Police arrived and carted the unconscious men and their weapons away. I sat in a chair and looked shaken when an officer poked his nose in. I told him I was OK and the loan officer had just fainted. When he was gone, Salome and Bart and Gus joined me again, invisible.

Salome said, "All the robbers are in the bank except the getaway driver. He's already gone. Left when the police arrived, I guess."

"OK. wake up the loan officer, Salome, take your papers. Bart, take us home, please."

Half an hour after we got back to the office, a detective visited me. He wanted to know what happened at the bank. I told him the truth. An associate and I were at the bank getting some papers notarized. A bunch of robbers in masks stormed in and shot a guard. Two of them took the manager to the vault and after he opened it they shot him too. I and my associate used our psychic powers to put the robbers to sleep and fixed the two men who were shot. You're welcome."

Detective Andersen, a nice young man who was clearly out of his depth, said, "I need you to come to the station and give us a statement."

I handed him the typewritten statements of myself and Salome. I said, "We're busy, so we prepared these statements for you. There is no mention of our deeds in there and I won't go to the station with you. If you made any records of what I just told you the defense attorneys would get the charges thrown out. Magic is not well accepted by the judicial system.."

He persisted and said, "I'm going to arrest you and take you in so my boss can hear your story. They certainly won't believe me."

I replied, "On what charge. I didn't rob the bank. And as far as I know, its not a crime to be present at a miracle, is it? And I'm not a viable witness. Once I told anyone how I saw what I did, my testimony would never reach a jury." I didn't tell him there was an invisible wizard standing behind him.

He saw my logic and stood up to go. I said, "I was glad to help. If the Seattle PD ever needed help with a serious situation, just call. We were available at a ridiculously low rate. Oh and we can keep a confidence."

After work I invited everyone to come to my house for a celebration. Everyone came. I even invited Millie's new assistant. Her name was Alicia and I was sure she wouldn't spread tales about our merry crew. Her brother, Michael operated a Native cuisine restaurant in Rainier Valley. A local gang had threatened him because he wouldn't pay their protection racket. The police were aware of the racket, but couldn't get any evidence or witnesses to appear. Alicia told Michael about us. She was in a Native American book group with Millie and heard of our PI skills. He agreed, so Alicia told Millie about his problem. I agreed to 'relieve his problem' and just charge him for expenses. I didn't like scum preying on hard working folks.

I gave Michael a burner phone with a speed dial for my phone. He was to press the number one when any of the gang came to his restaurant. I briefed Gus and Bart and gave them the location of the restaurant. A couple of days later I got a call from that burner phone. I told Bart the gang's thugs were at the restaurant. He was standing behind them before they said a word. Bart and Salome talked to them and they identified all the gang members and their victims.

I talked to that nice Detective Andersen and he gave me the department's data on the gang members. I told him I was going to convince them to go away with no violence. He was glad to help.

Bart took the whole gang to a warehouse I rent in South Seattle. We had hung pictures, names, addresses and vehicle descriptions of all of them on a wall. He showed them that he and Gus were not only bulletproof, they were taking over their territory. The gang was given twenty four hours to leave the area or told they would vanish without a trace. Bart sent them home and they were not seen in Seattle again.

Miguel was not told what happened, just that they wouldn't be bothered by that gang again. Millie had talked to Alicia and found they were members of the same tribe and Alicia had an accounting background. Millie wanted to hire her and I knew she needed help, so, now she's one of us.

I talked to Bret and he said he'd be there. He was in Europe, but there was no reason to stay tonight. Bart jumped us all home from the office.

Bret had lined up some drinks on the kitchen table I didn't recognize. He held up one for my inspection. He said, I recall you liked the absinthe we had in Casablanca. This is a aquavit made in Hoodsport. by The Hardware Brewery. Local by your standards. It has an anise and cardamom flavor. He poured me a small amount.

It was good. I said, "Local eh? I would like some more please." He poured and picked up his glass and put his arms around me. Our kiss was hot and we cut it way too short in deference to our guests.

We set out pizza, snack, a veggie platter and drinks. Bart, Salome, Gus and I regaled the others with our day's activities. It was turning into a nice party. I put on some music and we danced on the porch for a while then we went back into conversation. We had just started talking about Bart and Salome's plans. Their house, babies, pets and all the usual things when there was a knock on the door. For once, Lucifer was the first one there. I didn't usually see him move so fast. Alicia was the first human to the door. She opened it and Horus ran past her into the room. He stopped and looked around. I think he was confused by having two girls with enchanted rings in the same room. Poor guy, he whimpered and wandered back and forth between Salome and Esmerelda.

I saw Father Magnus and waved him in. "Good evening, Father. Have you found you missing Sister Hancock yet?

He looked unhappy and said, "I know where she is, but she won't let me exorcise the demon. Says she is having too much fun. Jesus let her down and she's making up for him with his evil win."

I saw Salome grin in my direction. Little did she know what Bret and I did.

"So, Father," I asked, "why are you here?"

He said, Horus led me here. He thinks there's a demon amongst you."

Where was Horus? I looked around and found him in a corner with Lucifer. It looked like they were talking quietly. I guess that's OK.

I replied, "Father, he's right, but I don't think the people involved are interested in having him exorcised."

Salome said, "That's right Father. Asmodeus is quite useful to me."

Esme said, "Me too, sorry. I want to keep him."

Father Magnus said, "But he will taint your immortal souls. You will bear his imprint in the afterlife."

"Father," I said," I don't think so. We're using him to help people and staying faithful to our loves. Just what Jesus would want. We're not letting lust make us unfaithful, but to enhance the lives of us and our loved ones. We can handle the temptation better than others could. You should go find Sister Hancock. She's using pure lust to tempt strangers in her new role as Dana Danger in a strip club.

He left, muttering to himself, reluctant to leave any trace of the demon behind, but we wouldn't budge. We had to push Horus out the door after him.

The party wound down and I took Bret up to bed, anxious to play with my wizard, my magic man, my master.

The End

Kindle Titles by Alan Horn

Total Control 1
Total Control 2
Total Control 3
Submissives
Wage Slaves 2
Pony Girl Sentence
Consequences
Julie
The Coffle
Coffled Future
Coffle Cure
Laura's Key
Laura's Coffle
Pony Girl Dreams
Honor & Obey
Ensnared
The Love Ring
A Natural Slave
Humiliation
Bad Iris
Good Iris
Brave Iris

Printed in Great Britain
by Amazon